Littpin & The Battle of Rockhill

OrangeBooks Publication

Smriti Nagar, Bhilai, Chhattisgarh - 490020

Website: **www.orangebooks.in**

© Copyright, 2023, Author

All rights reserved. No part of this book may be reproduced, stored in a retrieval system, or transmitted, in any form by any means, electronic, mechanical, magnetic, optical, chemical, manual, photocopying, recording or otherwise, without the prior written consent of its writer.

LITTPIN & THE BATTLE OF ROCKHILL

ABHIJITH CHANDRA

OrangeBooks Publication
www.orangebooks.in

DEDICATED TO

*Amma, Achan, Menaga, Vicky,
My friends and my readers.*

Foreword

I still remember the time when we were having a random conversation in the corridor, and I mentioned my book "Teen Ache" and the next thing I knew, he started working day and night, and the end result was an entry into a magical world "Korangeera". Again here he is, all set to release his new book "Littpin & The Battle of Rockhill"...When his imagination and creativity merge with the power of ink, the characters in the imaginative world are given a touch of reality.

Dear readers, the author has expressed his intense desire to see his imagination brought to life on the big screen one day, and I suggest that when you read this book, you visualise each scene in your mind and let us hope that in the future we are in for a visual treat as well. I have read the first book, "Korangeera", and it was beyond my expectations of a debut novel, so this time, I know what I am delving into. Waiting to grab a copy.

Dr Shreyas Susan Varghese

Jubilee Mission Medical College.

"My greetings and best wishes to Mr Abhijith for his second fiction novel, "Littpin & The Battle of Rockhill"... I'm sure Abhijith's ideas and imagination will continue to enthral readers across the spectrum."

Lenin V. Toppo I.A.S.

Telangana Cadre

Acknowledgements

This book is my second stepping stone into the world of fiction, and I am thankful to Almighty for making the path clear without any obstacles and blessing me with lots of friends and well-wishers.

First, I will start with my parents, K.V. CHANDRAVASAN (Retd. Sub Inspector of Police, Kerala) and K. SARASWATHY, who have supported me in this journey and on all other journeys. They have never tried to curtail my imagination and restricted other relatives from entering my personal space with unnecessary questions.

My Big brother ABHILASH CS (Infosys, Belgium) and his wife KRISHNAPRIYA (FedEx, Belgium) supported and motivated me throughout the process. Also, it is my brother who, after reading my first book, suggested increasing the number of pages in my next book. (Two more people also told the same, which I will describe later)

Next is my all-time all-weather companion MENAGA V. I.F.S. (Ministry of Environment, Forest & Climate Change, Government of India), Without whom my imagination would have never blossomed. She is the one who told me to pen down my imagination, which got later published into my firstborn "Korangeera". She also criticised my earlier book for not having many pages along with my brother. Also, she wanted me to include more plots in my next book, and I hope I have done it. More than Six years of togetherness with her have inspired me to create two characters, Kutty & Littpin.

Now, the third person who criticised my earlier book for not having many pages is one and only Reshma Radhakrishnan. A pure critic of my earlier book, even in the drafting stages. The earlier book would have ended badly without her, especially in the last chapter. I was planning to stop by the second last chapter, but she said, "Every book should have a climax, and you shouldn't disappoint the readers by just putting a question mark". Even in this book, I kept that in my mind and was happy that she liked the book once she completed the first draft.

The tripod of my life, my three best friends, Amal Krishna (Dell technologies), Kiran SS (Cognizant), and Aravind R(Asst. Director, Film Industry), who was a staunch believer of my creations, be it Korangeera or Littpin. Their support and motivations inspired me to write more. They are the first persons who read my earlier drafts, and I will send the manuscript to the publisher only if they are satisfied with the storyline. They won't praise my work unless it is good, so I trust their feedback and will make the necessary corrections. So I am blessed with a tripod which supports me in all my ventures.

Dr Shreyas Susan Varghese, aka SSV, is a name I will never forget in my literary world. She is the first author I have met and informed me about self-publication and its procedures. Without her, the stories of kutty, Korangeera, Littpin, Singali, etc., wouldn't have been published as a book; instead, they would have remained idle in my creative world. Her continued support throughout the process of my first book helped me to launch "Korangeera" successfully. So in this book also, I wanted her imprints, and she did the foreword of this book.

Next is Athira S. Kumar I.R.S., a close friend who has supported me since we met. During her interview preparation, I launched my first book Korangeera and even during the peak time of her preparation, she anchored the book launch function. Now in the busy schedule of her job, she read my book and wrote advance praise for this book.

Rev.Fr.Saji Mekkattu (Administrator, IAS HUB), my mentor with whose support I am standing here, launching my second book. This journey would have been difficult if he had not supported me. And in this book, a character named "Sajeera" is inspired by him.

The Rail Bureaucrat, Dr Krishna Muthu Rajan I.R.P.S., my close friend who had appreciated me a lot for my first book, and he was eagerly waiting for the second book. When some of my friends criticised me for the reduced number of pages in korangeera, Krishna had a different view. He said the book was an easy read, and there are good books with fewer pages.

I also warmly thank my classmate Lenin V. Toppo I.A.S., Who had wished me great success in my literary journey.

For every literary work, language is essential to convey emotions, and Aiswarya Sudha helped me improve my book's language; after her touch, the book's quality lifted to new heights. She wasn't just editing; she understood the plot and added proper punch throughout the book. There was a huge difference when I compared my first and final drafts; all credit goes to her.

Next is Shijin Mathew, without whom the book cover page would be some random image of a Rockhill. With his sound creative mind, I got a beautiful Cover page that portrays the last battle scene. Also, the interior pictures are part of his creative work. I was very impressed when he drew the cover page, and I told him when this book is made into a film, he will be the art director.

Nancy Maria has provided the material support with her i7-powered laptop for the cover page design. It would have been a more challenging job for Shijin and me if she weren't there.

Ashwin Mathew and Adarsh B. Uday, the duo team at IAS HUB, have read the earlier draft of this book and pointed out necessary corrections, which helped me to reduce the mistakes. During the writing period also, they have enquired about the process and speaking with them kept me rejuvenated, which helped me add more plots.

Also, I would like to warmly thank Kavya Nair PJ, Vrindha V Thulasi, Aiswarya Krishnan (Roshini) and Malavika for supporting my literary works.

The honest reviews of Swetha Jain I.R.P.S. and Nikita Agrawal I.R.P.S. helped me improve this book's storyline.

Also, I would like to thank Sarath Pattambi (Director, LEAD IAS), Anuroop Sunny (Senior Academic Consultant, LEAD IAS), and Mohammed Shinas (Director, Ilearn IAS) for their direct and indirect support in this journey.

I also thank Devipriya Ajith I.F.S., who helped me gift the first copy of this book to Menaga.

Lavanya B. I.R.P.S. gave me a detailed list of corrections and suggestions regarding my first book. And keeping that in my mind, I tried my best to avoid mistakes in this book. I want to thank her for her honest review.

Next, I would like to thank Vishnu Gopi, who found time to draw a picture for this book, which we can find in this book where the story ends, "The Rockhill and the Valley side". I was happy when he showed me the sketch; it looked exactly like what I had in my mind.

Abhirami S., Nizam Shahal (Kerala police), Ribu.C.Daniel, Diba V. Jacob, Nebic Johnson, Flora Elsa Mathew, Ananthakrishnan KV, Yedhukrishnan, and all my friends, teachers and relatives, I thank you very much for the support and wishes.

And finally, I thank the interior designer of my book at Orangebooks, whose name I still don't know, also Madhvi and Payal, all of whom helped me launch this book successfully.

Advance praise for Littpin & The Battle of Rockhill

"An indeed gripping thriller that keeps you glued to your seats till the very last page . Get ready to skip a heartbeat or two !".

Athira S. Kumar I.R.S.

Customs and Indirect taxes

Message from the Author

Dear readers,

I am excited to launch my second fiction novel, "Littpin & The Battle of Rockhill". I request all my readers to read "Korangeera" first and then read this book, as these two are part of the same Series. I hope I could be able to satisfy your expectations.

INDEX

Chapter 1
The Feast 1

Chapter 2
Boom Yaay 5

Chapter 3
The Mysterious Stable man. 14

Chapter 4
The Outlaws 17

Chapter 5
The Clash of the Chiefs 22

Chapter 6
Sarparna Sthabdh 28

Chapter 7
The Sorcerer of weapons. 32

Chapter 8
The Night Rider. 37

Chapter 9
The Mind voices. 41

Chapter 10
The Dream 46

Chapter 11
The Conspiracy 49

Chapter 12
The vow of silence 54

Chapter 13
Missing in Action 56

Chapter 14
The Sky is red and blue 59

Chapter 15
Into the fireball 62

Chapter 16
The Heat waves. 66

Chapter 17
The firefly 69

Chapter 18
The Trident 72

Chapter 19
The mighty Vaani Sena 77

Chapter 20
The uninvited guest 80

Chapter 21
Gone fire gone 84

Chapter 22
The Serpentines 87

Chapter 23
The King Cobrython 91

Chapter 24
The Revenge of Cobrython. 95

Chapter 25
The Proud Brother 103

Chapter 26
Lost and found. 106

Chapter 27
The Rogue soldier. 109

Chapter 28
And their watch ends. 112

Chapter 29
To the Palace 117

Chapter 30
The Commander 120

Chapter 31
To Malnat 125

Chapter 32
The Climb 128

Chapter 33
The cool breeze 133

Chapter 34
The Beautiful Capital City 136

Chapter 35
The Recruitment 139

Chapter 36
Abheera 144

Chapter 37
The Outlaw Spies 147

Chapter 38
The Reunion. 150

Chapter 39
The Rescue 155

Chapter 40
Ammu 158

Chapter 41
Truth alone triumphs. 166

Chapter 42
The Night jokes. 173

Chapter 43
The Search 176

Chapter 44
She is free now. 179

Chapter 45
The Chief of Security. 183

Chapter 46
Lord Manikta 185

Chapter 47
The Sheep Eater 190

Chapter 48
The beggars 194

Chapter 49
Battle Ready. 197

Chapter 50
Vengeance Vs Justice 202

Chapter 51
The first wave. 206

Chapter 52
Don't look up 209

Chapter 53
The Battle of Rockhill 212

Chapter 54
The Scroll 218

Chapter 55
The Last Wave 223

Chapter 56
Chief Ashwadarsh 230

Chapter 57
One last fight. 234

Chapter 58
The Airborne 238

Chapter 59
The Blue 244

Chapter 60
The Visions 253

List of Characters. 263

The Rockhill & The Valleyside. 264

Korangeera – Praise 266

Chapter 1
THE FEAST

Across the window covered in glistening dew drops, Littpin saw the rising sun smiling at her; She longed to smile back at it but was too weary even to unlatch her eyelids. The Golden sun warmly lighted Littpin's room, and she realised she couldn't sleep anymore as her father may barge in anytime. As expected, someone opened the door.

He possessed a well-built, hairy physique adorned with numerous scars, and among those scars rests a sizeable chain around his neck, with an eagle claw hanging down. He stared at her and shouted "Littpin".

Littpin jolted awake and saw her father's fiery red eyes staring at her. She was silent, her gaze lowered, her eyes fixed on the ground as she braced herself for her father's reprimand, unsure of which mistake had caused his anger. Such was the mischievous nature of Littpin. Memories of the previous night flooded Littpin's mind.

Last night Littpin and her father Venkad attended a banquet hosted by the ruler of Tamnat, a province within the Bharatha country renowned for its bustling market where people from far and wide gather to trade. Venkad, who serves as the chief of trades and possesses expert knowledge of weaponry, received an invitation to the feast due to his esteemed position in the council. Being a food enthusiast, Littpin eagerly joined her father. Unfortunately, upon arriving late, the gatekeepers refused to grant them entry to the premises.

Gatekeeper: Sorry chief, the Lord's orders. Latecomers are not to be allowed inside.

Venkad: Even a chief is not allowed inside?

Gatekeeper: chief, this is a strict order from the Lord.

Muthu, who had joined them, grew agitated and appeared ready to confront the guard, but Venkad intervened, halting his younger brother's hot-headed impulse. Although Muthu was Venkad's sibling, he possessed a short fuse, a trait absent in his level-headed older brother.

Venkad said, "Muthu, we are outsiders, and they will always keep that in mind".

Muthu replied, "But we are also serving the land with our hard work; we are providing them with medicines and supplying the best weapons for the Vaani Sena, so how could they discriminate against us?"

(Vaani Sena is the armed force of Tamnat meant to protect the merchants and the land. Their military prowess was so highly regarded that they formed an entire battalion in the army of the Bharatha king Vasaraya.)

Venkad said,

"Muthu, whatever we do for this land, they will always consider us outsiders, and we have done the same for Vanyanadu.....".

Venkad stopped abruptly, and his eyes started filling with tears. Seeing this, Littpin interrupted and asked her father

"Father, I am so hungry".

Venkad burst into a laugh; he said

"We got no feast today. Let's go home and eat some fruit."

Her spirits dampened as she realised the anticipated feast was now out of reach. However, the quick-witted Littpin came up with an idea. She lay on the ground and started crying.

Venkad asked her what this was about, to which she replied

"Father," she explained through her tears, "I am hungry, and mere fruits won't satisfy my hunger."

Venkad understood her plan and boarded the horse cart, paying no heed to Littpin's words. Littpin burst into loud sobs, but her father remained oblivious to her true intentions. Unaware of Littpin's plan, Muthu approached her and inquired,

"Littpin, what do you want?"

Littpin replied, "Let's go to the city Center and buy the meat meals from the wine shop."

Muthu, who was initially unaware of her plan, now grasped what Littpin was attempting. "The shops might be closed now," he suggested. "Let's return home." Muthu joined Venkad inside the horse cart.

Littpin realised that her scheme to enjoy a sumptuous meal had fallen through. She picked herself up from the ground and reluctantly entered the cart, fatigued from the exertion of her drama. Then, a new idea came to her mind. She pretended to fall asleep in the cart, and when they arrived home, Venkad lifted her gently and carried her to bed, unaware that she was merely putting on an act.

Chapter 2

BOOM YAAY

A thud on the door brought back Littpin from long-forgotten memories.

Venkad asked her, "Littpin, what are you hiding under the cot?"

Littpin was shocked and replied, "nothing, father."

Venkad inquired, "So, what's that moving object under your cot?"

Littpin peered under her cot with great anticipation and was struck with disbelief as she saw a mysterious object moving under it. Covered with a cloth, she struggled to identify what it could be. Her mind raced with possibilities - could it be an animal, a trapped bird, or something else entirely? The curiosity was overwhelming.

Despite her playful and childish behaviour, she displayed commendable courage as she approached the cot and pushed it aside. Suspecting that the moving object was long and narrow, she removed the cloth to reveal a strange and unfamiliar item that left her astonished. Stepping back in surprise, she realised she had never seen anything like it before.

What truly caught her off guard, however, was her father's reaction to the object.

Venkad leaned against the door, grinning at Littpin, who was puzzled by his lack of surprise. She wondered why he was smiling until she looked up and saw the object hovering in the air, not on the ground.

Suddenly, Venkad exclaimed, "Happy birthday, my dear!"

Littpin realised that it was her seventeenth birthday and that her father had gifted her something special, as he always did on her birthday. The previous year, he had given her a stunning dagger adorned with a red gemstone, which she cherished and carried with her at all times.

Littpin asked father

"What is it, father? I haven't seen such an object, which is entirely new. Why is it airborne? What will I do with it?"

Venkad smiled and replied, "I don't know whether you are excited or curious about the gift. But I was hoping for a thank you first."

Littpin apologised,

"I'm sorry, Father. I am both excited and curious, and I forgot to thank you."

She rushed to her father and gave him a tight hug. For Littpin, her father Venkad and his brother Muthu were the only family she had ever known. She had never met her mother, who had passed away during childbirth. Ever since then, Venkad had played the role of both a father and a mother, showering Littpin with love and affection. Perhaps it was this pampering that had made her mischievous and playful.

Littpin continued hugging her father. Venkad patted her shoulder and said

"It's a flyer, dear."

Littpin asked inquisitively, "Flyer? Does that mean I can fly this thing?"

Venkad responded affirmatively, "Yes, my dear. You can fly it."

"Boom, yaay" Littpin shouted with excitement.

"but on one condition," said Venkad.

"what is it, father?" Littpin asked.

"You should not fly around market place or near the Vaani Sena, and also, you should not fly far away into deep jungles," said Venkad.

"Then where should I fly this, father?" Littpin asked satirically.

Venkad laughed and said, "you could fly this around our home, grasslands, mountains, and even along the edge of the forest."

"So, I cannot show this to my friends also, right father?" Asked Littpin.

"No, you cannot", replied Venkad.

"Why should I keep all the gifts a secret? Even the last gift, the dagger, I always kept it under my clothes." Littpin took a deep breath.

"One day you will get to know dear", replied Venkad.

Littpin approached the Flyer, and she ran her hand over its smooth surface, feeling the strange markings etched into it. To her, it resembled a long shaft but with a tapered front end and a boxy back end that was polished to a shiny green finish. Littpin was surprised that she could even see her reflection in it. As she examined the Flyer closely, she noticed a foldable saddle attached to its mid-portion, adding to the mystery of the strange device.

Littpin asked her father, "Father, how did you get this?"

Venkad replied, "Dravas gave it to me, my dear".

Littpin was puzzled and intrigued by her father's response.

"But father," she asked, "how could Dravas uncle have given it to you if he's in Malnat? You haven't visited Malnat for years. Also, if it is transported from Malnat, the Vaani Sena would have checked it at the border and would not have allowed it inside." Said Littpin.

Hearing this, Venkad's eyes were filled with tears, not because he was sad but because he was proud of his daughter analysing facts and giving judgments, a quality much needed for a princess.

Venkad kneeled down beside Littpin and placed his hands on her shoulders.

"My dear Littpin, Dravas gave this to me a long time ago, and your mother was with us when she made those markings," he explained with a soft and nostalgic tone.

Littpin's heart felt heavy with emotions, and she couldn't help but let her tears fall. She felt a strange connection with the markings, as if they were a message from her mother, a message that she couldn't decipher. Littpin grew up not knowing much about her mother, as Venkad was always tight-lipped about her. Muthu would occasionally tell her stories, but they were few and far between. This is the first time her father has said something about her mother.

Littpin gently traced her fingers over the markings on the Flyer, feeling the smooth surface and trying to decipher their meaning. As her tears fell on the markings, they seemed to shimmer and glow in the light. Though she couldn't understand the markings, Littpin felt a deep sense of connection to her mother and the love that had gone into creating this special gift for her. With a heavy heart, she closed her eyes and held the flyer close, feeling its weight and warmth against her chest.

Overwhelmed by emotions, Venkad went outside to the courtyard and gazed at the breathtaking view of the rising sun. As he stared at the horizon, memories of the past flooded his mind, and he couldn't help but feel a heavy weight on his chest. His legs trembled, and he collapsed onto his knees, his head hung low as tears streamed down his face and moistened the ground beneath him. With a deep breath, he was lost in his sea of flash memories.

"A helpless mother bathed in blood holding two children closely…." Venkad's flash memories were interrupted by Muthu, who was trying to lift Venkad. Muthu, who was a mighty warrior, didn't find it hard to lift Venkad, but the sight of his elder brother's pain weighed heavily on his mind.

Muthu said, "I know it's hard, brother, but those memories weaken you, and you have to let it pass".

Venkad replied, "What should I forget, Muthu? She drew her final breath in my arms. Should I forget that? They came to our homeland, destroyed our forests, poisoned our waters, and killed our clan members.

Should I forget that too? Tell me, Muthu, what should I forget?"

Muthu empathised with his brother's pain and tried his best to provide some comfort to him.

"I understand how difficult this is for you, but we must be strong and face whatever challenges come our way," he said, wrapping his arms around Venkad in a warm embrace.

Venkad splashed his face with the cool, clear water from the nearby stream, hoping to wash away his sorrow. The glistening river seemed to offer a sense of solace as if it understood his pain. But his moment of respite was cut short when he heard the piercing scream of Littpin in the distance. Without a second thought, he bolted towards their home, his heart racing with fear and concern.

Littpin and the Flyer were lying on the ground, and Muthu was holding her legs. Knowing what had happened, Venkad could not stop his laughter. He said,

"My dear, please forgive me. I forgot to tell you one thing".

Littpin stared at her father and asked, "what now?"

Venkad said, "The flyer will work only in sunlight, dear".

"Father….!" Littpin yelled.

Muthu, who was massaging her legs, fought hard to keep a straight face. He knew Littpin all too well and was afraid that if he laughed, she might kick him.

Muthu carried Littpin inside, and Venkad accompanied them. Littpin asked Muthu to serve breakfast as she was hungry after the fall.

As they sat around the breakfast table, the scent of freshly cut fruits and vegetables filled the air. The steam rising from the hot vegetable soup made it look like a mini volcano on the table. Venkad and Muthu, who followed a vegetarian diet, were content with their food. Littpin, on the other hand, had a longing for meat, which was not on their menu.

After breakfast, Muthu rushed to the stable to prepare the horses for their ride toward the council meeting while Venkad went to his room to change the dress.

Venkad's wardrobe was not ordinary. It has a vast collection of body armour, swords, boots, helmets, daggers, etc. He had shiny body armour for official council meetings. In council meetings, the chiefs mostly wear shining armour rather than combat ones. They carry shining golden swords and daggers, purposefully to show their wealth and power. Some chiefs who are wealthier even carry heavy golden weapons that are useless in combat.

Venkad is a warrior, unlike other chiefs who were wealthy nobles. Even when Venkad uses shining armour in council meetings, he always carries his combat sword and dagger.

He tightened his armour and placed the sword and two daggers in his sheath. His sword is unique, with a beautifully crafted eagle pommel. The blade is sharp and is made of no ordinary steel. And his daggers weren't as lengthy as the standard daggers.

Venkad made his way toward the stable and spotted Muthu feeding the horses with grass. His temper began to rise as he knew that the task of feeding the horses should have been completed much earlier in the day.

Venkad shouted, " Muthu, where is Virumen?"

"There he is", Muthu pointed towards the corner of the stable.

Virumen is the stable keeper of Venkad. Along with Virumen, there are four guards to keep their home safe and a maid, Sugandhi.

Venkad glanced at Virumen, who was seated in the corner lost in contemplation.

Chapter 3
THE MYSTERIOUS STABLE MAN

Virumen is a reserved individual who rarely engages in conversation and spends much of his time lost in contemplation. Littpin finds Virumen's peculiar mannerisms unsettling and often feels intimidated by him. Virumen constantly carries a dagger and occasionally fixates on it for hours on end. The dagger in question bears visible blood stains.

Venkad has always ignored Littpin's questions about Virumen. She somewhere knows there are so many mysteries related to Virumen nevertheless she gets no answer from her father or her uncle.

Venkad went to Virumen and took the dagger from his hands. Abruptly, Virumen rose to his feet and made a respectful gesture as if he had just surfaced from deep contemplation.

Venkad patted Virumen's shoulder and said;

"Some memories will stay with us until our death, but we mustn't let those memories drown us".

Muthu looked at Venkad with grief. He is aware of the immense emotional distress that talking about past memories would have caused Venkad, acknowledging that it is often difficult to let go of one's past.

Littpin also joined them at the stable. She saw Venkad consoling Virumen but decided not to interfere with them. Approaching the stable, she observed the four horses alongside two carts - one of which was open while the other was heavily armoured. Amongst the horses, three were a shade of brown, while the fourth stood out, being a striking white colour named Veera.

Littpin's equine companion, Veera, is held in high regard as he stands out from the other horses in many ways. While his legs lack the bulk of the other three, his blue eyes resemble the vastness of the ocean, and his tail isn't as fluffy as the others. Despite these differences, Veera's agility surpasses that of his peers. He possesses a deep understanding of Littpin's moods and adapts his behaviour accordingly. In moments of sadness, Veera takes the reins and steers Littpin towards the hills, knowing that they are her favourite spot. Despite being under Virumen's care at the stable, Littpin herself takes responsibility for Veera's well-being.

The other three horses are masculine, and they look like war animals with solid legs and long sharp teeth. They are looked after by Virumen. Because of his strict training, these three horses are very much disciplined.

As Muthu began to prepare the two brown horses for riding, one of them suddenly bucked and displayed aggressive behaviour with a loud neigh. However, within moments, the horse settled down. Littpin glanced towards Virumen and was frightened by the intensity of his gaze fixed upon the unruly horse. The animal itself seemed to be intimidated by Virumen's fiery glare, which caused it to quickly calm down.

Littpin murmured,

"what a mysterious man?"

Venkad and Muthu started their journey toward the city centre.

Chapter 4

THE OUTLAWS

In order to reach the city center, they must traverse through a forest whose dense canopy blocks even the sun's rays. Venkad urged Muthu to hasten their pace, as the forest is known to be perilous - not only due to the presence of wild animals but also due to the threat of outlaws who prey on unsuspecting traders and travellers passing through.

While travelling at top speed, their progress was abruptly halted by the sound of a woman's cries for help. Muthu and Venkad raced in the direction of the voice in search of the Woman, only to find that the entire forest had fallen silent. The Woman's cries had ceased, causing Venkad to signal for caution as they continued their search.

Amidst the Woman's renewed sobs, a harrowing sight came into view - the Woman was bound to a tree with thorny chains, her naked body bearing numerous cuts from a bladed weapon. Venkad realised that the Woman had been subjected to torture and sexual assault by the outlaws responsible for her captivity.

Venkad cautioned Muthu: "They might be somewhere near us, be prepared."

Both of them drew their swords and monitored the surroundings, detecting some approaching movements. They assumed defensive stances as four men emerged from the foliage and rushed towards them. It was Muthu who saw it, and he shouted

"Poisoned swords...."

At the sight of their swords, Venkad observed a slick film covering the tips of the blades.

He knew it was dangerous to combat with them closely as even a minor cut would be fatal. With remarkable speed, Venkad hurled his daggers at the outlaws in a boomerang-like trajectory, penetrating their hearts before returning to his hand. The remaining two bandits were astounded by this display and surrendered by dropping their weapons.

After asking Muthu to tie them, Venkad approached the Woman and untied her. He removed his body armour and asked her to wear it.

Seeing this, Muthu asked:

"Brother, what are you doing? How can you give away your armour?"

"Muthu, is it right to leave her unclothed? Her honour is of greater importance than my well-being. At present, she requires it more than I do," replied Venkad.

"But brother…"

"No, Muthu. It's crucial to prioritise aspects of our lives. Upholding the dignity of women in our community is paramount. When a woman is content and provided with opportunities to grow, the nation prospers. We all know the story of Arasar, right?"

The outlaws hung their heads in guilt, their eyes brimming with tears.

Seeing this, Venkad asked them.

"How could you do such a heinous crime? Don't you think about your mother, sister, wife, and daughter? What if this same situation happens to them?"

Both of them started sobbing.

Venkad looked at the Woman. She held her palms together and bowed down with immense respect toward Venkad.

She said: "My Lord, from this day to the end of my life, I will never forget your kindness and your words. I have never seen anyone with so much respect toward women. Most of the men consider women as slaves, but you, my Lord…" she started crying.

Approaching her, Venkad placed a comforting hand on her shoulder and spoke, "Lady, I am not a lord. I am the chief of trades at the Lord's court."

"You may not be a lord for others, but for me, you are my lord", she replied thankfully.

Realising that his brother was right, Muthu's mind was filled with joy and pride. Upon listening to the Woman's words, he recognised his mistake in opposing his brother's decision to give the armour to her.

The outlaws continued to weep, and one of them uttered

"My Lord, we are guilty of our mistakes. Please give us a befitting punishment."

Venkad looked at them; he said,

"I perceive that you both feel remorseful. Nonetheless, I am not in a position to dictate the consequences in this circumstance."

Venkad pointed to the Woman and said,

"Lady, today you are the Goddess of justice. Give them their punishment for the crime they committed against you."

She replied: "My Lord, I don't want to punish anybody. I have suffered the pain, and I don't want to give it back to them. I see remorse in their eyes, and I forgive them."

Her ruling left everyone stunned.

Muthu untied the outlaws, and they approached the Woman and bowed in respect. Drawing their knives, they sliced their palms and pledged an oath.

"My lady, from this day to the end of the day, we serve to protect you."

Both of them approached Venkad and bowed down.

Venkad said: "From today onwards, you are not outlaws; you are Soldiers,". He gave his two daggers to them as a token of respect. The daggers were not made of steel and were very lightweight. They respectfully kept the daggers in their sheaths.

'Now it's time to depart; we will surely see each again in the cycle of time' saying this, Venkad and Muthu scaled on their horses and resumed their journey.

The Lady and her soldiers bowed and said goodbye to their Lord.

Chapter 5
THE CLASH OF THE CHIEFS

Tamnat is a prominent as well as a vast region, and its most notable locality is the City Center, which houses the Palace of the provincial Lord. Upon reaching the entrance gate of the city, Venkad and Muthu were greeted by the gatekeepers, who saluted them and opened the gate. As the grand gate slowly opened, the two of them made their way into the city.

The Bharatha King selects the Provincial Lords from amongst his loyalists. While the present ruler of Tamnat, Rakarna is a Just leader, and he is constantly under the influence of Marutha, the head of Medicine, who manipulates him.

Marutha is the brother of Rakarna's wife and a highly skilled physician renowned as one of the best in the country. However, his ego poses a problem; whenever someone bruises it, he seeks revenge by manipulating the Lord. His ego-driven actions have led many to be ostracised into the forests, where they become outlaws due to the complex circumstances.

Soldiers of Vaani Sena and the people were shocked to see the chief of trades without armour. The Captain of the gate guard inquired about the matter from Venkad, who then briefed him on the story. After hearing the details, the Captain saluted Venkad, which once again filled Muthu with pride for his brother. Besides being a sibling, Venkad serves as Muthu's role model, mentor, and trainer.

Captain asked: "Shall we proceed to the council meeting, chief?"

"Yes, Captain", replied Venkad.

Venkad, Muthu, and the Captain, accompanied by five soldiers, started walking towards the meeting hall of the Palace. As Venkad approached the entrance to the meeting hall, he observed a small group of soldiers from the king's army stationed nearby.

Venkad asked the Captain:

"Captain, why is the king's army stationed here?"

"Chief, don't you know?" Asked the Captain.

"What is it, Captain?" Venkad asked in surprise.

"The General of the King's army is here". Captain replied.

"Oh, that's something big! What is the purpose of his visit, Captain?" Venkad enquired

"Sorry, chief, I don't know," Captain said.

Upon entering the hall, they discovered it was empty. The Captain inquired with the gatekeepers and learned that all the chiefs had gone to the Palace stable to see the General's horse, which had been bitten by a snake during their journey. Consequently, they also hastened to the stable.

The sight was distressing as the black stallion wailed in agony, and General Atheendra was nowhere in sight, presumably far enough to escape the reach of his horse's mournful cries. The Chief of Medicine and his aides were administering treatment to the horse, but to no avail. Venkad noticed an unusual occurrence since Marutha's medicines would typically work immediately upon application.

Venkad approached the horse and examined the bite wound, causing him to be stunned by what he saw. He glanced at Muthu, who joined him and examined the wound as well. Muthu grasped Venkad's hand and inquired softly, "Are they here? In Tamnat?"

"Might be," Venkad replied.

Amidst the commotion, a voice rose above the clamour, that of the Chief of Medicine, Marutha. He instructed the soldiers to disperse the gathering, allowing only the chiefs to remain present. Marutha then informed Lord Rakarna that the poisoned leg needed to be amputated to prevent the poison from spreading any further. Rakarna consented to the removal of the ailing horse's leg.

Venkad interfered, "No, don't do that. There is no need to amputate the leg".

Venkad's statement irked Marutha, and he retorted with anger,

"Am I the chief of Medicine or you, Venkad? I know what I am doing. So please do not disturb my work here. I have to save this horse."

"You are not saving this poor animal. We need not amputate him. Marutha, I am not disrespecting your work or expertise", said Venkad.

"Oh, is that so? Then what should we do, Chief of Trades? Should we trade him? Tell me, I am listening", Marutha was fuming with anger.

Venkad understood that Marutha's ego had been bruised, rendering him unwilling to listen, thus leaving the helpless creature to suffer in agony. Venkad was aware that he was the only one capable of saving the horse as the snake that bit the animal was not of a typical breed found in Bharatha country. Knowing what to do, he signalled Muthu to provoke Marutha. In response, Muthu began disparaging the Chief of Medicine, asserting that he had failed to save the General's horse and was unfit for the job, which is why he is arguing with his brother Venkad.

"How dare this outsider bastard challenge me in front of the Lord of Tamnat Rakarna." Marutha retorted with anger.

Muthu unsheathed his sword witnessing which Marutha's guards drew their swords, causing a chilling silence to descend upon the onlookers. However, this did not affect Venkad and Muthu as they were confident that their plan was proceeding as intended.

The news reached General Atheendra's ears, and he came to the stable. All the soldiers bowed, seeing the General. He ordered the men to drop their arms. Atheendra looked at Venkad and asked Lord Rakarna about the incident. After knowing what happened, the General asked Venkad,

"Chief, what can we do to save my horse?"

The General's response was unexpected, as he directed his query to Venkad, even though the Chief of Medicine was present beside him, leaving everyone taken aback.

Venkad replied, "General, we must melt a particular alloy into the wounded to stop the poison from spreading".

General approved Venkad's method, and Venkad took his sword and melted the blade's tip using the heavy flames which Muthu prepared. Venkad slowly poured the molten alloy into the wounded portion of the leg. The horse started crying louder, and Venkad murmured something in his ears. The horse slowly calmed down, taking everyone by surprise.

Marutha said, "An alloy to treat a snake bite, it's madness".

And to their surprise, the horse rose again, jumped, and made a loud neigh.

"Yes. My boy is back," shouted the General with happiness.

Venkad approached Marutha and whispered in his ear,

"If I see your ego working again, I will crush your skull and chop you into pieces of meat."

Marutha didn't utter a word, he was already shocked to see the horse getting healthy, and Venkad had the General's support now.

Everyone was happy seeing the poor horse standing again. They praised Venkad. The General approached Venkad, hugged him, and said

"You saved my boy, Venkad. I owe you for a lifetime for this help."

Venkad said with humility: "It is my duty to serve the people, animals, and forests".

General smiled at Venkad and asked Venkad to meet him at his chamber. Venkad and Muthu followed the General. Afterwards, the other chiefs resumed their duties while the black beast contentedly consumed its feed.

Chapter 6
SARPARNA STHABDH

Venkad and Muthu attended the council meeting following their meeting with the General. The members discussed various matters like trade, security, and relations with neighbouring provinces such as Malnat. That is when Venkad raised his concerns regarding the issue of protection within the forest area, but he was met with mockery by the other council members.

The Chief of Security, Ajral, mockingly said, "You are worried about the security inside the forest since you lost your body armour". Hearing this, everyone started ridiculing and laughing at Venkad. Venkad remained calm, but Muthu was fuming with anger. Venkad said to Rakarna, the Lord of Tamnat,

"My Lord, it is crucial that we protect the forest area as the outlaws are becoming more aggressive and unpredictable with each passing day."

The Lord Rakarna inquired, "Venkad, do we really need to do that? Deploying Vaani Sena in the forest will be an added expense to the treasury. Moreover, I believe we already have sufficient security on all the city borders."

"My Lord, I urge you to consider deploying at least a platoon of soldiers at the entrance of the deep forest area. It is essential to isolate the deep forest from the rest of the woods." Venkad's concern is not about the outlaws who have been present in the forest for years, but something else, which was apparent from his facial expression.

By seeing the tension on Venkad's face, Lord Rakarna said,

"Let it be. I will deploy thirty soldiers for the forest area. There will be a Captain for the platoon, and you will be the Commander in charge."

Despite being aware that these thirty soldiers may not be sufficient for the impending threat, Venkad was still grateful for the additional security. However, he cannot confide in anyone regarding his concerns, as they will not believe him until they witness it firsthand. This is precisely why Venkad requested a platoon of soldiers to witness something unprecedented, which the people of Bharatha country have never experienced before.

The meeting was dispersed, and all the chiefs departed to their homes. Venkad and Muthu went to the barracks to meet the platoon's Captain.

Venkad instructed the Captain to equip his soldiers with only light body armour for their mission inside the forest. When asked about the reason, Venkad replied,

"Captain, we are not facing ordinary soldiers inside the forest. Heavy armour will only slow us down, and we need to move swiftly like lightning to handle the forest terrain and the enemy efficiently."

"Okay chief, I understood. And what about the weapons, Is there any particular specification?" Asked the Captain.

"We need some modifications, Captain, but we cannot do it here. We will do it at my place." Replied Venkad.

"Chief, shall we meet our soldiers?" The Captain asked

"Yes, Captain, let's meet the brave men of Vaani Sena", said Venkad with pride.

They marched towards the parade ground, where the thirty soldiers arranged themselves in three rows of three soldiers each. As their Commander-in-Charge, Venkad, arrived, they saluted him promptly. Each soldier was equipped with heavy armour and a long sword hung in a sheath on their left hip, with a dagger on their right hip. They were entirely prepared for battle, representing the elite Vaani Sena.

Venkad addressed the elite force with his inspiring speech,

"Warriors of Tamnat, today is a historical day for me. Today I was bestowed with the charge of thirty brave men of Vaani Sena—the most lethal force in the country, the elite force with an impeccable performance record. We need to fight an enemy in the deep forest, and I know you are our best option. Soldiers, today we March to the forest, and our war cry will be "Sarparna Sthabdh".

Soldiers, in unison, shouted the war cry

"Sarparna Sthabdh, Sarparna Sthabdh..." Despite being unaware of the significance of the war cry, they began marching towards the forest land.

Chapter 7
THE SORCERER OF WEAPONS

The marching party ventured into the forest, and they eventually arrived at the edge of the dense woodland. Venkad instructed the group to stop and take a break, allowing the soldiers to rest for a moment. While seated on a large rock Venkad, Muthu, and the Captain engaged in a weighty conversation. Venkad took a piece of cloth and began sketching a map of the forest, outlining areas for the soldiers to be stationed at the entrance points of the deep woods. It was emphasised that no soldier should venture into the heart of the forest, a command that the Captain readily agreed to.

Captain asked Venkad,

"Chief, what about the weapons? Shall we start making it?"

"Yes, Captain, we must go to my home to make it," Venkad said.

The Captain delegated control of the platoon to a soldier, and they set off towards Venkad's residence. They arrived at Venkad's home close to nightfall, where Littpin was eagerly anticipating Venkad's return. Upon hearing the sound of horses, she hurried to the stable and embraced Venkad tightly and started crying.

Venkad asked, "what is it, my girl? Why are you crying?"

Littpin remained tearful and didn't utter a word, and Venkad didn't probe further. He respected her need for space and allowed her to have it.

Venkad took off his sword and rested it on the horse's saddle before picking up Littpin and carrying her towards her room. Muthu and the Captain shared a smile as the heartwarming scene showcased the deep bond between a father and his daughter.

Venkad placed Littpin in her bed and kissed her forehead, and said,

"My dear, I know you are disturbed, and you don't have to tell me why. But remember one thing; I will always be there for you."

Hearing this, Littpin started crying further. Venkad left the room as he knew she needed time and space alone.

Venkad proceeded to his room and retrieved a round object from a metal box. He then made his way to the weapon workshop, which was located far from the stable and home. Venkad took such precautions because he didn't want the people living in the house or the horses to inhale the harmful smoke generated during the weapon-making process. Venkad was a considerate person whose love and concern for others, as well as animals, were unparalleled.

Muthu and Captain were already waiting at the workshop for Venkad's arrival. Muthu had already begun melting the iron. Upon Venkad's arrival, he handed the round object to Muthu, who proceeded to place it into the fire, increasing the intensity of the flames.

The Captain asked, "What is that material, Muthu?"

"It is an alloy from our place, captain, and the intensity of fire has to be very high to melt it." Replied Muthu.

The Captain refrained himself from inquiring further about the material as he respected the need for secrecy. If the material had not been confidential, Muthu would have gladly provided an explanation. The Captain caught Venkad's gaze, and Venkad responded with a warm smile.

He appreciated the Captain's honourable character and complimented him, saying,

"You truly are a gentleman soldier, Captain."

The Captain didn't reply and just smiled back at Venkad. Both of them looked at Muthu. He was focused on his work and started mixing the iron and the alloy. There was a massive reflection of fire when the molten iron and alloy were combined.

They closed their eyes due to the intense reflection. And the reflection persisted for a little time. After it had reduced, the Captain asked the reason for this intense reflection.

And Muthu said,

"Whenever this alloy is burned and is in contact with any other metal, an intense reflection will be produced."

And the Captain nodded his head like a student listening to his teacher.

Muthu's craftsmanship was evident in his work. The core and outer parts of the sword were made of alloy, while the other parts were iron. It was made so as to ensure that the alloy was efficiently used to give the sword its strength and sharpness.

After seeing this, the Captain asked,

"Will there be any problem if we make the entire sword with that alloy?"

Venkad and Muthu looked at each other and started laughing. Captain was confused.

Muthu said,

"Captain, there is no problem in making the entire sword with this alloy, but the problem is we don't have that much alloy to make a full alloy sword for the entire platoon."

The Captain now comprehended the reason behind the sword's composition of both iron and alloy, and he was amazed by Muthu's skilled craftsmanship. Muthu had strategically utilised the alloy to enhance the blade's strength by incorporating it into the sword's central region. Additionally, to improve the sharpness of the blade, he had employed the alloy on the outer edges. The result was a "sandwich" of alloy-iron-alloy, which was an impressive feat of sword-making.

The Captain's inner voice whispered in admiration,

"What a remarkable weapon, crafted by such a skilled smith; he is truly a sorcerer of weapons."

Chapter 8
THE NIGHT RIDER

After completing the first one, Muthu gave Virumen the directions to make the remaining swords. Virumen is also an expert in weaponry and training.

Venkad told the Captain,

"Captain, after the completion of all swords, Virumen will deliver the weapons to the soldiers. It will take the whole night to make all the needed weapons, and you can stay here for the night. We leave by tomorrow."

The Captain gave a nod, prompting Venkad to instruct Muthu to prepare the cart for transporting the weapons. As Venkad and Muthu departed the workshop, the Captain bid farewell with a salute and made his way to his designated room.

Meanwhile, Venkad checked on Littpin and found her fast asleep. He covered her with a blanket, closed the windows, and retired to his own room. Exhausted from the day's events, Venkad fell into a deep slumber as soon as he lay down on the bed.

At around midnight, Littpin abruptly woke up with a troubled expression on her face. She clasped both her ears tightly as if trying to block out a loud noise. However, there was no sound to be heard. She surveyed her surroundings and opened the window to let in some fresh air, but it didn't seem to calm her down. Eventually, she left the room to find Veera.

Although Veera was sound asleep, he woke up at the sense of Littpin's presence. When she reached him, he made a small noise and nuzzled her. Littpin hugged him tightly, stroking his soft fur. She repeated this gesture a few times before signalling for Veera to go back to sleep. Despite her insistence, Veera remained by her side, sensing her distress.

"Okay, I understand, but we cannot go outside now," Littpin told Veera.

Veera neighed and lowered his back to assist Littpin to mount. Veera took Littpin for a ride inside the compound. The Captain, who was sound asleep, woke up by hearing the whinnying of Veera. He opened the window and saw Littpin riding Veera. He was surprised to see Littpin riding a horse at midnight. He thought to himself, "What happened to this girl? "... There might be something disturbing the poor girl. Earlier also, she was seen crying, but the chief didn't ask much about it also. Maybe she is missing her mother. Who knows what her problems might be, poor girl." The Captain closed his window and went back to bed.

Littpin was considerate of Veera's potential to disturb everyone's sleep, so she brought him to the stable and gave him some attention before leaving. As she exited the stable, she noticed smoke emanating from the workshop. Having already sensed that something significant was happening due to the presence of a platoon Captain and her father, she headed towards the workshop to investigate.

Upon arriving, she saw Virumen working on the lathe, with finished swords being stored in an open iron box nearby. Despite noticing Littpin's arrival and her troubled expression, Virumen continued to work without speaking to her.

Littpin came near the iron box and took one sword. She tried the basic strikes with it, and she realised the perfectness of the sword; it was not heavy like the iron swords.

Virumen was watching all this, and he asked,

"Mind voices?"

Littpin just nodded and kept the sword in the iron box, and went to her room. She sat on her reclining chair and slowly slipped into deep thought,

"Sometimes he speaks, sometimes he doesn't. But he understands things very clearly. He is a clever man, but something happened to him, don't know what it is. He might have lost someone very close, like I lost my mother. But I haven't even seen her. I never got the love of a mother, father always tries his best to make sure that I don't miss her, but still a mother is a mother...." Gradually, she drifted off to sleep.

Chapter 9
The Mind voices

In the morning, Venkad was awoken by a loud thud. When he opened his window, he realised that he had slept soundly through the commotion of Virumen and Muthu loading the iron boxes of swords onto the cart. Quickly, he took a bath and prepared himself for the ride to the forest.

As he made his way to the courtyard, he encountered the Captain, who saluted him and asked:

"Chief, yesterday I saw your daughter riding the horse at midnight. She was very disturbed. What happened to her?"

"Captain, she is fine and solid now. Sometimes she hears mind voices during her sleep, which keeps her disturbed." Replied Venkad.

"Mind voices?" Asked the Captain.

"Yes. And it's not a big deal, Captain. She will be okay in no time." said Venkad.

Although the Captain had a sense that Venkad might be concealing something, he refrained from inquiring further due to his position as Venkad is both the superior officer and chief, and out of respect for Venkad's privacy.

Together, they made their way to the transportation cart, where the Captain proceeded to inspect one of the iron boxes and check the sword inside. Muthu reassured the Captain by saying,

"Don't worry, captain. It is perfect," and grinned while winking his eye.

"No, Muthu, I was just curious to see it again and wasn't checking the quality. Your craftsmanship was proved yesterday itself." Said the Captain.

"I was just pulling your leg, Captain", and he started laughing.

Approaching the Captain, Venkad took the sword from him and began to swing it expertly, leaving the Captain surprised by his impressive display of skill. From the stable, Littpin observed the scene while feeding Veera his morning meal. She eventually made her way over to Venkad and simply gazed at him in admiration.

Venkad placed a comforting hand on Littpin's shoulder and asked,

"How are you, my little eagle?" He had a habit of referring to her as an eagle whenever he felt a strong sense of affection towards her.

"I am excellent and ready for a battle, father," she said.

"Then let's have a battle, my dear," Venkad said.

Venkad threw the sword in his hand to Littpin, and she caught it perfectly with a swift body movement. The Captain was shocked again.

"How can a seventeen-year-old girl make such a quick move," he thought.

Venkad selected another sword from the box, and the two began to swing at each other in a friendly bout. Though Littpin was his daughter, Venkad did not hold back, confident in her abilities as a skilled sword fighter that he had trained himself. Littpin's body was remarkably agile and supple, allowing her to execute quick and nimble manoeuvres during the fight.

After the fight, the Captain gave them a standing ovation. Muthu felt proud after seeing the Captain's reaction.

Venkad told Captain,

"Cap, I told you my girl is solid."

"Yes, chief, there is no doubt." Replied the Captain.

Muthu placed the swords from Venkad and Littpin in the box. Venkad hugged Littpin tightly and said,

"I am very proud of you, my girl."

"All credit goes to you, father. You are the one who believed in me and trained me to become a fighter like you are," said Littpin.

"Not like me, more than me." Said Venkad.

Venkad looked at Muthu and said,

"Muthu, now I can die peacefully, right?"

"What, brother…?" Muthu asked with an angry face.

Littpin's face turned red, and she rushed to her room; seeing this, Venkad also felt saddened.

He instructed Virumen to pack the boxes tightly and told Muthu and Captain to begin their journey to the forest. And Muthu asked,

"Brother, you are not coming?"

"I will catch up with you. Now I have to speak with Littpin; she is slightly stressed." Said Venkad.

"Not slightly, brother. You shouldn't have spoken like that in front of her." Said Muthu.

Venkad nodded his head in agreement. The Captain saluted Venkad, and they started their journey towards the forest with a cargo of new weapons for the soldiers. Meanwhile, Venkad proceeded to go and see his angry daughter.

Chapter 10
THE DREAM

Littpin's room was locked from the inside. Venkad knocked twice, and Littpin opened the door and sat on her reclining chair. Her face was still red with fiery red eyes. Venkad approached her and knelt down beside the chair. He said,

"My baby, I didn't mean to hurt you. I was saying that I was happy. As a daughter, you have fulfilled my dreams, and that is what I meant dear." Tears roll down from Venkad's eyes.

Littpin wiped her father's tears and held him by his cheeks. She said,

"Father, do you know why I cried yesterday? I had a terrible dream, and you know what it is? In that dream, you died, father...." Littpin's voice was broken as she completed these words.

Venkad held Littpin's hands, which were resting on his cheek, and reassured her with a tender voice,

"Don't worry, my dear. It was just a dream, and it won't come true. So, please try to relax. I will always be here for you."

"Father, a dream is something we experience, even if it's not real. So, its impact can still be significant," said Littpin, expressing her concerns. "You don't know how it feels," she added.".

"My dear baby, I have experienced more than a lifetime's misery. These dreams are nothing but our fears. You love me a lot, so you fear losing me, and that is why you had such a dream, baby." Venkad consoled Littpin.

"Okay, Father. Thank you so much for easing my pain,"

Littpin conveyed her gratitude to Venkad. Venkad wanted to change the topic and bring a smile to her face. He asked about the Flyer he had gifted her. He was guilty for not being able to spend much time with her on her birthday. However, he assured her that he had made all the arrangements at home to make her happy, even instructing Sugandhi to cook her favourite meat dishes.

"Father, the Flyer is fantastic. It makes me feel weightless, and I can go wherever I please. It's marvellous," said Littpin.

"I'm glad you liked my gift, baby. Would you like to take a ride to the forest?" asked Venkad.

"Wow, it would be so much fun to fly with you," Littpin replied.

"No, no. Not in the Flyer. We'll take the horse cart. The Flyer can't support my weight, dear," Venkad explained.

"Then let's tie Veera to the cart, father. He'll be delighted to see the forests," Littpin proposed, and Venkad agreed.

Venkad and Littpin worked together to tie Veera to the cart, and they were both overjoyed. As they set out on their journey, the guards saluted Venkad and opened the gates for them. However, Venkad soon realised that he had forgotten to bring his sword.

"Wait here, Littpin. I need to grab my sword. I forgot to bring it," Venkad said, halting the cart.

"Father, let's just take a sword from the guards and keep moving," suggested Littpin.

Not wanting to disappoint his daughter, Venkad asked one of the guards to lend him a sword. He then kept the sword in the cart as they continued on their journey. With Littpin hugging him from behind, the father and daughter duo enjoyed the ride. Veera leads the cart with happy neighs.

Chapter 11

THE CONSPIRACY

"Father, why has there been a sudden deployment of troops from the Vaani Sena inside the forest?" asked Littpin. She had been curious about it since yesterday but had only found the time to ask about it now.

"Nothing to worry about, dear. It's just a usual protocol. The army will station there whenever there is a security breach until the threat is dealt with." Replied Venkad.

"What is the threat, father? The outlaws?" Asked Littpin.

"Yes, dear, you are such a brilliant girl." Said Venkad.

"But Father, the outlaws were already in the forest, committing petty crimes. What is this new threat that has led to the deployment of the Vaani Sena?" asked Littpin, still curious. Venkad was pleased with her analytical skills but was unsure of how to respond.

"Usual military protocols, dear." Venkad hesitated to explain further.

Littpin was aware that her father's excuse was a cover-up for something significant happening in the vicinity, as he wouldn't have utilised the unique alloy to forge swords for the stationed army otherwise. This realisation led to another question that had been bothering her since the previous day.

After overcoming her apprehension, Littpin asked her father,

"Father, I couldn't help but notice that you returned yesterday without your daggers and body armour. I wanted to inquire, but I was too preoccupied with my dream. Can you tell me what happened?"

Venkad responded, "It's a long story, my dear, and I will share it with you in detail when we get home today. Is that alright, my baby?"

Littpin agreed, "Sure, Father. However, I'm curious, how did you lose your favourite daggers?"

Venkad smiled, "No, my dear, I didn't lose them. I gave them to someone deserving who will utilise them well."

From then on, they travelled in silence, each with their thoughts, providing each other space to contemplate them.

Upon covering some distance, they arrived at the temporary barracks established by the soldiers. Muthu and the Captain were resting against the cargo cart, which had not been unloaded yet, anticipating Venkad's arrival to distribute the swords. Spotting Venkad approaching, Muthu and the Captain hurried towards the cart.

The Captain saluted Venkad, and Muthu greeted Veera with a pat. Littpin also hopped out of the cart. Venkad instructed the Captain to assemble the troops. The Captain blew the horn, and in a matter of moments, all the soldiers had gathered in formation.

Venkad directed them to stand at attention. He took a sword from the iron box in the cargo cart and exhibited it to the soldiers. The soldiers were taken aback by the new blade and its distinct colour shade. Venkad informed them about the advantages of the alloy mix and instructed Virumen, standing beside the cart, to demonstrate to the soldiers how to keep the swords in top-notch condition.

Virumen showed the soldiers how to sharpen the sword and store it when not in use. After Virumen's demo of sword maintenance, Venkad ordered the Captain to distribute the weapons to all soldiers.

Swords were distributed, and the soldiers started swinging their new weapons. They praised the design and material of the new blade. It gave them more confidence, strength and pride.

The soldiers were then instructed to return to their individual outposts. Afterwards, Littpin untethered Veera and gave him food and water. While Littpin was occupied with something else that bothered her, Venkad,

Muthu, and the Captain conducted inspections of all the outposts.

Once Venkad returned from his tour, Littpin approached him and queried,

"Father, do you notice the three soldiers stationed near our cart?"

"Yes, dear, I know what you are going to say. They are not skipping their duty; now they are off duty and will join their duty by evening." Replied Venkad.

"No, father, I am not talking about that. I feel something wrong. They have been speaking secretly beside our cart since the moment you left for rounds, and it seemed like a serious discussion. And I feel they are up to something." Said Littpin with a tense face.

"No, dear. You are overthinking. And the soldiers of Vaani Sena will never be a part of any conspiracy." Said Venkad.

Disagreeing with her father's assessment, Littpin became upset. She went back to Veera and caressed him. Venkad perceived that Littpin was angry because he didn't consider her observations. Nevertheless, Venkad was aware of the Vaani Sena and their training, recognising them as one of the top forces in the country, leaving no cause for scepticism.

However, Venkad was also perplexed since Littpin possessed exceptional observational and analytical skills.

Hence, if she detected an issue, it was plausible that something was indeed amiss.

Venkad was in a dilemma now, and he thought to himself,

"Are those three part of a conspiracy?"

"If yes, what might it be?"

"What is there inside this forest to conspire for?"

"Will there be a mastermind behind it?"

Venkad called for the Captain and ordered him to watch those three soldiers. The Captain reluctantly nodded as he had faith in every soldier in his platoon.

Chapter 12

THE VOW OF SILENCE

On her way home, Littpin entered the other cart which Virumen was riding. Venkad and Muthu were travelling in a smaller cart with Veera tied to it. Venkad knew that Littpin was still angry, and it would take some time for her to calm down. He felt sad that Littpin had vowed to be silent with him.

Veera, sensing the sadness of both Littpin and Venkad, let out a low whinny, and tears rolled down his eyes. Venkad's cart slowed down, and he gently patted Veera's back, understanding the weight on his mind. He didn't force Veera to speed up.

Muthu sensed something amiss between father and daughter but didn't want to make Venkad sad by asking about it. Meanwhile, Littpin's mind became heavy, torn between her anger towards her father and her desire to speak with him. Tears flowed down her face like a rushing river, and she wiped them away, staring straight ahead at the road.

Virumen felt the heaviness inside the cart, and he realised it was not because of the empty iron boxes.

They reached home, and Venkad gave back the soldier's sword, and he went to his room with a heavy heart. He could lift a mountain, but he couldn't handle Littpin's vow of silence.

Littpin saw her father walking with a heavy heart. She wished to go and speak with him, but she couldn't. Littpin was driven mad by the dilemma. Since they had arrived home, Sugandhi had been observing her closely. Knowing Littpin's character well, she asked,

"Littpin, I know you want to talk to your father. What's stopping you?"

Littpin didn't say a word and instead hugged Sugandhi tightly. With her mind made up, Littpin decided she was ready to speak with her father.

Chapter 13
MISSING IN ACTION

As evening approached, the Captain gave orders for the soldiers to take on duty shifts. Among them were the three soldiers who had been accused of conspiracy by Littpin. With everything seemingly in order, the Captain retired for a nap.

Upon waking, the Captain directed the soldiers to place torch lights at all the outposts. Two soldiers fetched the torchlights from the barracks and installed them.

However, they later informed the Captain that two torches were missing. Despite this, the Captain appeared unconcerned; he dismissed the missing torches as a minor issue, saying

"It's just two torches, perhaps they were misplaced. I suggest you thoroughly search the barracks to locate them."

The two soldiers returned to the barrack to search for the missing torches. And the Captain went inside his quarters and started having the meat soup prepared for him.

Out of the blue, two more soldiers arrived and signalled their arrival by ringing a bell outside the Captain's quarters. The Captain set down his soup bowl and stepped outside to meet them. The soldiers saluted the Captain and informed him that three soldiers were unaccounted for at a particular outpost.

The Captain was taken aback and asked, "Have you thoroughly searched for them?"

To which they replied, "Yes, Captain, we have combed the area, but they are nowhere to be found."

Captain rushed inside and took his sword, and came back. He told the soldiers to form a rescue party consisting of five soldiers to whom the Captain ordered,

"Soldiers, you must search everywhere and be prepared for an ambush; the outlaws are everywhere."

The Captain was apprehensive that if this was an outlaw attack, Venkad's residence might also be targeted. Only four guards, who were not even warriors, were stationed there. To prevent any potential danger, the Captain assembled a group of five soldiers and dispatched them to guard Venkad's house.

Meanwhile, search operations commenced, and the Captain convened the remaining soldiers for an emergency briefing.

"Soldiers, three of our soldiers are missing, and we assume we are under attack."

The announcement by the Captain that three soldiers were missing in action left the soldiers in disbelief. The elite Vaani Sena had never before experienced such an occurrence, and this was the first time a declaration of missing in action had been made.

The Captain then went on to explain that a search party of five soldiers had been formed to look for the missing soldiers, while another group of five was tasked with guarding the Commander's home, who had been attacked by the outlaws the previous morning. Despite their numbers being reduced to just seventeen, the Captain reminded the soldiers that they were still the mighty Vaani Sena, and their bravery on the battlefield was not determined by their numbers. This motivational speech stirred the soldiers' spirits, and they let out a resounding war cry.

"Sarparna Sthabdh"

"Sarparna Sthabdh"

Chapter 14
THE SKY IS RED AND BLUE

The Guard party has reached Venkad's home. Venkad was shocked to see a party of five soldiers of Vaani Sena at this time. Venkad came outside, and the soldiers saluted Venkad, and the leader of the party reported,

"Commander, we are under attack, so the captain has ordered us to guard here."

"Under attack? Who?" Venkad asked.

"The outlaws, Commander." Said the leader.

Venkad knows that the outlaws don't have the strength to attack Vaani Sena in an open battle.

Many thoughts lingered around Venkad's mind.

"Who will it be?"

"Is it what I have feared? Is it happening?"

"Then I must inform General Atheendra."

"Should I warn all the chiefs and lords of Bharatha?"

Littpin approached her father,

"Father, what is it?" Littpin's question broke Venkad's deep thoughts, and he said,

"We are under attack, and these soldiers have come to guard us".

"Guard us? Father, does the Captain think that the outlaws could do any harm to us?"

"My dear, an attack has already been reported at the forest outpost," said Venkad.

Littpin turned towards the leader of the soldiers and asked,

"What kind of attack was that soldier?"

"The Captain has declared three soldiers missing in action." Reported the soldier.

Littpin and Venkad looked at each other, and they, in unison, asked,

"Three soldiers?"

"Father, it might be them, the conspirators." Said Littpin.

Venkad nodded his head in agreement, and he asked the soldiers,

"Soldier, can you describe the looks of those three soldiers ?" Asked Venkad

"No, Commander, we don't know which soldiers went missing. The Captain formed this guard party when he got the report of missing soldiers." Replied the leader of the group.

Venkad called Muthu and Virumen and ordered them to get the horses ready. Littpin knows that Venkad is planning to visit the forest outposts to confirm whether the alleged conspirators are the missing soldiers.

"Father, I will also come." Said Littpin.

"No, my dear..." before Venkad could complete his words, there was a huge explosive sound which shattered everyone's ear.

The explosion sound was from the deep forests, and what they saw from their home was something they had never seen.

A vast cloud of smoke is coming from the deep forest, and the sky is filled with this smoke. They can see a reddish colour Amid the smoke.

Venkad said,

"Forest fire."

The fire and smoke have turned the sky Red and blue.

Chapter 15

INTO THE FIREBALL

The Captain was shocked by hearing the explosive voice. It took him a few moments to regain his composure and recover from the shock.

"It is a forest fire, and everyone cover your mouth with a wet cloth." Ordered the Captain.

The soldiers prepared for battle by wetting a piece of cloth and tying it around their mouths to protect themselves from the smoke. The Captain then gave the order to get ready for combat.

"We must act swiftly, soldiers. The forest fire could be a ploy by the outlaws. Our mission is to eliminate the threat," declared the Captain.

"Aye, Aye" shouted the soldiers.

"Leading party should guide the team. The tail party should watch if anyone follows us. And the middle party should look for any ambush coming towards us." Captain briefed the soldiers.

"Let's go, soldiers! Charge those bloody outlaws." Bellowed the Captain.

The soldiers fastened their lightweight body armour, secured the scabbard to their hips, and sheathed their swords.

They all shouted their war cry,

"Sarparna Sthabdh"

"Sarparna Sthabdh"

The group of seventeen soldiers headed by the Captain rushed towards the deep forest from where the fire started.

Venkad, Muthu, and the guard party readied themselves to venture into the deep forest. Following Venkad's instructions, they all covered their faces with wet cloths to protect themselves from smoke and other potential hazards. Muthu saddled the horses and even covered their mouths with damp cloths. However, Venkad did not permit Littpin to join them on their mission.

He said, "Littpin, we are going right into a fireball and are unsure if it is an ambush."

"But father, you have trained me very well," said Littpin.

"I have trained you, my dear, that's true, and you are a good sword fighter. But this is something new, very new. Even the Vaani Sena wouldn't have seen what was coming" Venkad stopped his words and ordered the ride into the forest.

Venkad has asked Virumen and the four guards to protect Littpin. Littpin was locked inside her room by Sugandhi and Virumen as per the directives of Venkad. Littpin was angry, sad and disappointed by this. But she is a warrior. She won't stop fighting. She sat on her reclining chair, scanning every corner of the room with her eyes, searching for a means of escape.

"What should I do?"

"Should I break the door? Virumen and Sugandhi will be out there?"

"Think, Littpin, think. You can do it?"

"I should have accompanied father."

"I couldn't speak with father properly after the forest visit. He must be sad about that. What if something happens to him? No, Littpin, don't think like that...."

"You should think about positive outcomes, no matter how bad your situation is."

So many thoughts lingered around her mind.

An idea suddenly came to her when her eyes fell upon the flyer that was tucked under her bed.

"Yes, I should make use of that. But my father told me that it would work only during day time. So, it won't fly now." Littpin was disappointed.

But Littpin was very clever, and she looked at the lamp lit at the corner of the room.

"If the Flyer works only in the daytime, light is important. And if I give the flyer proper light, it can fly, right?" Littpin thought.

Littpin took the lamp and increased the intensity of the flame, and she attached it to the boxy back side of the Flyer. She sat on the saddle and tried to lift it.

Littpin let out a loud "Yes!" as she carefully adjusted the Flyer, making sure it was suitable for the current lighting conditions. With a dagger, she began to dismantle the blocks obstructing the rooftop, creating a path for her Flyer to pass through. Once the path was clear, she lowered her Flyer and grabbed her sword and the dagger that Venkad had given her on her sixteenth birthday. She also equipped herself with lightweight armour.

After making these preparations, she took off quickly and headed towards the raging forest fire, just as her father had advised, charging straight into the fireball.

Chapter 16
THE HEAT WAVES

The soldiers led by the Captain had entered the deep forest, only to find that the situation was much worse than they had anticipated. While the Vaani Sena had been trained extensively for open-field battles and close combat, navigating the forest terrain was proving to be a difficult task. The smoke and intense heat were only making matters worse.

Realising the dire situation, the Captain ordered the team to halt and take a break. The soldiers were exhausted, finding it hard to breathe with their mouth wraps now dry. The Captain instructed them to wet the cloth again and take a moment to rest.

As the Captain removed his own mouth wrap, he noticed blood stains on it, indicating just how serious the situation had become. Looking around, he saw that his soldiers were also experiencing nosebleeds. Despite these challenges, the soldiers did not complain and were ready to continue their mission.

Filled with pride for his troops, the Captain sought to boost their morale and prepare them for what lay ahead.

He then gave an inspiring speech

"Brave souls, this is not the first blood. When others shed tears and sweat, we, the Vaani Sena, shed blood, and that is our identity—an identity which no superpower can erase. Yes, we are the mighty Vaani Sena, and we will win this battle. Let the invincible Vaani Sena rise."

"Aye, Captain", they shouted together.

"Rise, soldiers; take your arms, and let's make them bleed."

All the soldiers shouted the war cry together and marched forward.

"Sarparna Sthabdh".

"Sarparna Sthabdh"

"Sarparna Sthabdh"

"Sarparna Sthabdh"

Their war cry echoed amidst the heat waves.

As they continued to move forward, the intensity of the heat waves increased, causing some of the soldiers to disobey the Captain's direct order to keep their body armour on. Despite the Captain's warning not to remove their armour, most of the soldiers decided to shed their armour due to the extreme heat. Not wanting any protection that his soldiers didn't have, the Captain also removed his body armour.

Despite being without body armour, the soldiers marched forward with confidence, knowing that their strength lay in their minds and not in their bodies or weapons. As they approached the source of the forest fire, the Captain reminded the soldiers to be cautious and prepared.

Chapter 17
THE FIREFLY

As Venkad's team entered the forest at a rapid pace, they soon reached its edge, where all the outposts were found to be abandoned. Venkad was not surprised by this, as he had anticipated it.

He thought to himself,

"The Captain should have stationed at least two soldiers at the outpost to prevent isolation from the outside, maintain communication with reinforcements, and call for help if needed. Now they are completely cut off from the outside world."

Venkad then ordered two soldiers to guard the edge and instructed them to call for backup if they did not return by morning. He also advised them to hide in the bushes for camouflage.

The two soldiers chose a bush to hide in and followed Venkad's instructions not to engage in any combat, even if they encountered the enemy. Their role was to keep watch and report back to the Lord of Tamnat if no one returned.

Venkad and Muthu got off their horses and continued with the remaining three soldiers into the deep forest. The terrain was not suitable for horses, and they were also easily frightened inside the dense forest.

Muthu asked Venkad,

"Brother, what might have caused the fire?"

"It may be a built-up fire by the outlaws to trap the soldiers." Said Venkad.

"But brother, what if it is done by him?" Muthu asked Venkad.

"No, Muthu. He will never hurt the forest, and you know that. And if this fire is made by someone else, what we feared might happen." Said Venkad.

Suddenly something flew over their head.

"What is it?" Asked a soldier with awe.

No one in Tamnat would have seen such a scene in their lifetime.

"A bigger firefly", another soldier said.

Venkad and Muthu were startled by seeing this big firefly. They looked at each other, and Venkad's eyes were filled with tears.

"I am the reason for all of this,"

Venkad shouted, throwing his sword away. He kneeled and unwrapped the cloth around his mouth, and he cried,

"Bhuvinaaaaaaaaaaaaaaaaaaaa...."

The soldiers were shocked to see this. One of the soldiers picked up Venkad's sword and approached him. But Muthu stopped him and took the sword from the soldier.

"Brother, let's not waste time here. We have to get there quickly. She is in grave danger."

Rising to his feet, Venkad took the sword from Muthu and sprinted towards the deep forest, undeterred by the challenging circumstances. Muthu followed closely behind.

Although the soldiers also gave chase, they soon fell behind. This was not due to any lack of running ability on their part but rather because the mysterious object they had just seen was none other than Littpin in her Flyer with a lamp attached.

Had it only been a threat from ordinary outlaws, Venkad and Muthu would not have been so apprehensive. After all, Littpin was a skilled warrior who could easily defeat them. However, what Venkad and Muthu feared was something far beyond the imagination of the people of Bharatha. Even the mighty Vaani Sena wouldn't hold a chance against it.

Chapter 18
THE TRIDENT

When the Captain and the soldiers arrived at the location, they were met with the sight of numerous cave-like dwellings engulfed in flames.

These settlements had been constructed from a combination of leaves and twigs.

"This must be the settlement of outlaws."

"But who burned it?"

"No one will burn their settlements."

"Was it done by an outsider?"

The Captain was beset with many doubts, and as he took another step forward, an arrow hurtled towards him. However, he managed to evade it, and in response, he signalled for his soldiers to seek cover. They had already discarded their armour, making them more vulnerable.

The soldiers took refuge behind a colossal boulder and surveyed their surroundings. The Captain realised that they were still within range of the outlaws' bows and that any further movement would likely result in a volley of arrows. Due to the smoke and flames, they were unable to locate the archers.

He was taken aback when he examined the arrowhead and observed an oily coating on its tip.

"Poison", said the Captain. And he ordered his soldiers to stay put.

As he contemplated a new strategy for attacking the outlaws, the Captain realised that none of his soldiers would be able to move forward or backward without external support.

Despite this discouraging realisation, he refused to lose hope. He understood that, in order to achieve victory, a soldier must maintain an unyielding spirit. This was not just true for soldiers but for all aspects of life. A hopeful person will always find opportunities where others see only obstacles. The Captain was such a hopeful person.

Suddenly, a glimmer of hope appeared in the form of a light in the sky. The light grew closer with each passing moment until it was hovering over the settlements. It then descended gently to the ground in the midst of the settlements, where the archers were positioned.

The soldiers heard the sound of sword fighting emanating from the centre of the settlements.

The Captain thought,

"Who will it be?"

"Is that our missing soldiers fighting with the outlaws.?"

"Should I go and check?"

One of the soldiers told the Captain that the sword fighting had stopped, and he alerted that a footstep was approaching them.

The Captain told the soldiers to be prepared. As the sound of footsteps drew closer, the soldiers discerned that it was a solitary individual approaching them.

The Captain watched with bated breath as the figure emerged from the smoke. To his amazement, he saw Littpin approaching him in her lightweight armour, which was stained with blood. With each step, droplets of blood fell from her sword, creating a macabre trail behind her. She wiped the blood from her face and addressed the Captain.

"Captain, the air is clear; no more archers."

The Captain felt an immense sense of pride for the Commander's daughter. However, the battle was far from over. Suddenly, a horn sounded, but it was not from the Vaani Sena.

"Get your swords ready, soldiers," commanded the Captain.

The soldiers immediately formed a defensive formation and prepared for the impending attack. The air was eerily quiet, except for the crackling of flames. However, the soldiers detected movement in their immediate surroundings.

"They are coming," said a soldier.

"They are everywhere," said another.

The Captain and Littpin understood that the outlaws had encircled them, and they couldn't defend their present positions. Both Littpin and the Captain knew that the only way to survive this encircled attack is to take an offensive rather than a defensive position.

The outlaws finally revealed themselves, and their numbers were staggering. However, the soldiers did not falter, and they had faith in their Captain and Littpin, who had saved them from the archers through close combat. The soldiers shouted their war cry,

"Sarparna Sthabdh"

"Sarparna Sthabdh"

"Sarparna Sthabdh"

The outlaws stood their ground, but they did not immediately charge at the soldiers, which was unusual. It appeared as though they were waiting for someone to give them orders.

Littpin and the Captain looked for the leader of the outlaws.

The Captain remarked on the previous spy reports indicating the outlaws had no leader.

"However," Littpin pointed out, "if they truly lacked a leader, why would they hesitate to attack us now that they have the chance? It's evident they have someone giving them orders."

Captain concurred with Littpin's observation, and she gestured to him to prepare for an offensive attack. He instructed the soldiers to form a trident formation and await his signal.

Chapter 19

THE MIGHTY VAANI SENA

Upon seeing the Vaani Sena's trident formation, the outlaws quickly took up a defensive stance. However, the Vaani Sena charged towards them with swords raised. As they approached, the outlaws formed a circular formation to counter the trident formation.

Littpin and Captain remained unfazed and unpanicked as they had anticipated this defensive formation from the outlaws, and the trident formation was simply a decoy.

"Soldiers, Aalinga vyuh", ordered the Captain.

The soldiers abandoned the trident formation and transitioned into a hugging formation, which surrounds the enemy and crushes them from the periphery.

The enormous number of outlaws wasn't a problem for the mighty Vaani Sena. The outlaws raised their shields, but these weren't proper ones. It looked like makeshift arrangements. And many of them were mere wooden planks.

Captain and Littpin realised that the forest fire was not a trap set by the outlaws, as evidenced by their makeshift arrangements. It was either a natural fire or set by someone else.

The outlaws were not a regular trained army like the Vaani Sena. They were made up of farmers, weavers, scavengers, thugs and even included some nobles, traders, and soldiers. The Vaani Sena charged at the outlaws in a brutal attack, using their speed and powerful blows. It was like a thunder strike for the outlaws, who had never fought a regular army before, leaving their chances of survival against the mighty Vaani Sena at null.

Littpin fought like a true warrior, choosing to engage in sword fights only with the stronger outlaws, such as thugs and ex-soldiers, rather than the weaker farmers. Her fighting style was graceful, resembling a dance, but leaving behind a trail of blood instead of flowers on the ground.

"Littpin, watch your back", shouted the Captain, who was fighting with three outlaws simultaneously.

As Littpin kept a watchful eye on her surroundings, she noticed a large thug with bulging muscles and several nose and ear piercings. He wore heavy chains around his neck, and his long hair was a mixture of black and brown. Unlike Littpin's sword, his weapon was made of wood with a heavy metal attachment at the end.

The thug tried to strike Littpin with his weapon, but she was quick to dodge. However, when Littpin tried to attack back, he blocked her swift strike, leaving her astonished by his agility despite his bulky physique.

As their weapons clashed, their eyes locked in a fierce stare-down. The thug found it difficult to maintain eye contact with Littpin, and his hands grew weak as he stumbled backwards. Littpin's gaze seemed to possess a strange power that affected him. Despite his setback, the thug made another quick strike that caught Littpin off guard, sending her flying to the ground. With her armour broken and a piece of it piercing her body, she found herself bleeding and unable to reach for her sword.

As the big thug charged towards her, she searched for her sword but couldn't reach it. She observed Captain and the soldiers fighting fearlessly and crushing the outlaws, confirming that the mighty Vaani Sena was winning the battle. Though she didn't call for help, Littpin wasn't giving up without a fight and was ready to face death with her eyes closed.

Chapter 20

THE UNINVITED GUEST

Countless sounds reached Littpin- sounds of swords clashing, the thuds of outlaws falling, the war cry of Vaani Sena, the soldiers' shouts, and the footsteps of the approaching thug.

Her mind was filled with many thoughts.

"What will happen to my father after I die?"

"It will be tough for him."

"I haven't spoken to father properly since I took the vow of silence."

"I want to see my father."

"I want to speak with him."

Her mind was occupied by thoughts of her recent dream, in which her father had tragically passed away. The dream had been unbearable for her, as no one could endure the pain of losing a loved one, even in a dream. Even a strong and fearless warrior like Littpin had struggled to cope with the intense emotions it had brought forth.

She was always mischievous, and he liked it that way. Despite her mischievous nature, Littpin was not entirely happy. However, she did enjoy making those around her happy and keeping them entertained. This was why she often engaged in naughty behaviour.

Deep within her, there was a burning pain, like a fierce fire that never subsided. Littpin had never known the love and care of her mother, nor had she ever seen her. Unlike her friends in the city center who spoke of their mothers' cooking and scolding, Littpin had never experienced such things.

Nevertheless, Littpin loved her father deeply and knew that he had always tried his best to make her happy. He had even instructed Sugandhi to cook meat for her on her birthday, and he had trained her well in the art of warfare.

Despite this, Littpin was aware that her father had many troubles and nightmares. She had witnessed him crying on numerous occasions but had refrained from asking him about it. Perhaps he too missed her mother, she thought.

She also thought about her uncle Muthu, who always accompanied her father wherever he went. Muthu had always supported Littpin and played with her to keep her spirits up when she was sad. Even with his short temper, Muthu had never raised his voice in front of Littpin and had always shown her great care and affection. It was Muthu who had gifted her Veera, and Littpin was grateful for his love and kindness.

As her thoughts gradually receded, she once again became aware of the sounds of the ongoing battle. However, she realised that something was amiss - the approaching footsteps of the large thug were conspicuously absent.

"Where did he go?" Littpin spoke to herself, and she opened her eyes.

Tears started rolling down when she saw her father in front of her.

"Father,..." Littpin cried seeing Venkad.

As tears clouded her vision, she wiped them away and gazed at her father, only to be astonished.

Venkad stood there, drenched in blood, with his eagle pommel sword held aloft and blood trickling down the blade. The sword had impaled the thug's heart, and the body hung at the tip of the raised weapon.

The sight on the battlefield left all soldiers and outlaws stunned, causing the latter to retreat once they witnessed Venkad's fury. After dropping the thug's body, Venkad hurried towards Littpin and lifted her up. Slowly, he removed the armour pieces that had pierced her body and instructed Muthu to fetch medicine. Venkad applied a herbal remedy to the wound and secured it with a clean cloth.

Littpin continued to weep and hugged her father tightly, but Venkad gently pulled her away, knowing that she was in pain from the thug's attack.

"Father, I saw my death…" she couldn't complete the sentence.

And Venkad said,

"It's an uninvited guest, and it has to surpass your father to come to you, my dear."

Chapter 21
GONE FIRE GONE

The outlaws had all withdrawn, and the soldiers had once again demonstrated their skill, with no casualties among their ranks. The Captain instructed the soldiers to establish a perimeter and keep watch. He then hurried over to Littpin and exclaimed,

"It was an honour to fight alongside a brave warrior like you."

"I am also honoured to fight along with you, captain." Said Littpin in a lower tone.

Venkad guided Littpin to a sturdy and comfortable spot, instructing her to rest her body. He then directed two soldiers to keep watch over her and begin their customary inspection of the battleground.

During their sweep, they stumbled upon Littpin's damaged Flyer, which had been broken in half during the skirmish with the outlaws. Muthu retrieved the rear part of the Flyer, which included the attached lamp, and showed it to Venkad with a grin.

"Such a clever girl," said Muthu.

"Yes, she has got all of Bhuvina's traits." Said Venkad, his eyes filled with tears of joy.

The scene around the Flyer revealed twelve outlaw bodies, all of whom had been defeated in combat by Littpin. The Captain arrived on the scene and identified them as the archers. He added,

"Without Littpin, our victory would not have been possible."

Suddenly, a fierce wind swept through the area, extinguishing all the flames and plunging the forest into darkness. A heavy stillness filled the air.

"The war is not won". Venkad said in an alarming tone.

The Captain was alarmed by the tremble in Venkad's voice and immediately ordered the soldiers to light torches. As they lit up the area, the soldiers began to sense vibrations emanating from the ground.

"What kind of wind could make this forest fire extinguish in just a single blow?" The Captain asked.

Muthu looked at Venkad, and fear was evident on Muthu's face.

Venkad nodded his head and said,

"They are here, Muthu. The very thing we dreaded is coming?"

Muthu didn't utter a word, and he kept on looking at the bushes around the ground as if expecting something.

The Captain was unable to comprehend their communication and inquired,

"Who is coming here, Commander? The outlaws have already retreated, right?"

"Outlaws? No. It is not the outlaws, but something you have never seen, embrace yourself, Captain." Said Venkad.

Venkad recognised the urgency of the situation and realised he didn't have much time for a lengthy battle speech. He instructed the soldiers to chant the war cry loudly and without pause, although they were uncertain about the reason behind this request.

"Perhaps the chief has a particular motive for assigning this war cry to our platoon." thought the Captain. Because "Sarparna Sthabdh" was not the usual war cry of the Vaani Sena.

Chapter 22
THE SERPENTINES

Observing some movements beyond the bush, they lifted their swords and arranged themselves in a defensive stance. Venkad and Muthu positioned themselves close to Littpin while the Captain eagerly anticipated for the enemy's appearance.

"Snake, Snake,..." shouted the soldiers.

Out of the bushes emerged a colossal cobra, its neck expanding to form a menacing hood. This serpent was unlike any ordinary snake found in Bharatha country. Its size was larger, almost comparable to Venkad's, and its body scales were different, black in colour, resembling armour rather than normal snake skin. The Captain now understood why Venkad had insisted on a new weapon, as regular swords would not be able to even scratch this creature's body. He speculated that the Commander must have encountered and fought this creature before.

"But why didn't he inform me about the Cobra?"

"Even if he had told, I wouldn't have believed," thought the captain

"The General's horse may have been bitten by this cobra, and Venkad likely realised this at the time, which is why he requested for soldiers to be deployed in the forest," the Captain speculated.

Venkad, noticing the Captain's concern, signalled for him to remain calm.

The massive cobra began to advance slowly, eventually coming to a halt, leaving only fifteen steps between the soldiers and the Snake. Despite their fear upon seeing the enormous serpent, the mighty Vaani Sena held their ground without showing any signs of fear.

"Father, let's go home. We shouldn't stay here. Please, father, please," said Littpin.

Venkad patted her shoulder and said,

"This too shall pass."

"Father..." before she could finish her words, she was interrupted by a huge noise.

The outlaws, who had previously retreated, were now standing behind the giant Snake, and Venkad had come to understand the situation. It appeared that the snakes and the outlaws had a symbiotic relationship where the snakes protected the outlaws, and in turn, the outlaws kept the snakes isolated from the outside world, which is what the snakes desired.

Venkad ordered the soldiers to hold their ground and instructed them not to attack unless ordered to do so. The Captain was confused by this decision, stating,

"There is only one huge Snake, and we can easily kill it. Furthermore, the outlaws have already failed and won't stand a chance against us."

"Why is he not giving the order to attack?"

"There might be some reason; otherwise, he would have ordered it."

"Oh no. Are there more snakes.?"

Before he could think about it further, many more snakes emerged from the bushes, including red-coloured cobras. The soldiers instinctively took a few steps back, and even the Captain retreated. He contemplated giving the order to retreat as they were heavily outnumbered, and they now had to battle not only the outlaws but also these alien creatures. The thought of the many lives that could be lost in this battle made him consider whether anyone would even survive.

Littpin grabbed and pulled her father back and said,

"Father, give the order please…please give the order to retreat." she started crying by holding Venkad's hand.

"There is no going back, dear. The war had already started, and many lives were lost on their side. The war has to be completed." Said Venkad.

Venkad began to believe in Littpin's conspiracy theory that the three missing soldiers had burned down the settlements of the outlaws and the snakes. But the question remained, why would they do such a thing?

"It seems those soldiers have started a war with King Cobrython by attacking the settlements of the outlaws and the snakes. Now, he will have his revenge," Venkad pondered. He took a deep breath, preparing himself for the battle that was to come.

Chapter 23

THE KING COBRYTHON

Suddenly hissing, the leading Snake initiated an attack as both the outlaws and the snakes began to move towards the Vaani Sena.

"Stay..." said Venkad to the soldiers.

Despite being overwhelmed by the sudden turn of events, the soldiers managed to maintain their position. Venkad realised that he needed to uplift their spirits and signalled Muthu, who swiftly threw his daggers at the head of the lead snake, killing it instantly. Witnessing this impressive feat boosted the confidence of both the soldiers and their Captain.

The leader snake, known for its tough exterior, couldn't withstand the force of Muthu's swing. The other snakes and outlaws momentarily halted their advance, shocked at the loss of their leader. However, their pause was short-lived as another snake from the side took charge, and they resumed their attack.

With determination, Muthu and Venkad positioned themselves at the forefront of the formation and shouted in unison,

"Sarparna Sthabdh"

"Sarparna Sthabdh"

It was quite peculiar that the snakes paused briefly and then resumed, which surprised those present. As a result, the soldiers also began to chant their battle cry.

"Sarparna Sthabdh"

"Sarparna Sthabdh"

The snakes once again halted momentarily and resumed their movement, leaving the soldiers, and the Captain perplexed. It was then that they discovered that chanting their war cry, "Sarparna Sthabdh," caused the snakes to freeze in their tracks. The Captain realised that this was the reason the Commander had selected this particular battle cry.

Venkad and Muthu displayed remarkable bravery on the battlefield, fighting like seasoned warriors. Their combat skills were astonishing, and all the soldiers, the Captain, and Littpin were impressed. Within a short span of time, Venkad and Muthu had managed to eliminate almost ten snakes, which was a remarkable feat considering the circumstances.

While the soldiers engaged in combat with the outlaws, Venkad and Muthu focused on battling the snakes. Meanwhile, three soldiers were engaged in a fight with six outlaws near the bushes, and Littpin was watching the skirmish. Suddenly, a snake emerged from the bushes and attacked the soldiers, killing them instantly with its venomous fangs. Littpin was shocked and attempted to retrieve her sword, but the pain was too intense, and she collapsed.

As the number of snakes killed continued to rise, both the snakes and the outlaws were taken aback and withdrew into the bushes. The snakes had not anticipated encountering warriors as formidable as Venkad and Muthu on the battlefield.

After the retreat, there was an eerie silence that persisted for some time. Venkad instructed a wounded soldier to take Littpin back to their base, as neither she nor the soldier would be able to withstand any potential future attacks. Venkad was certain of this.

"I won't come without my father," Littpin told the wounded soldier who went to lift her.

"My lady, please come with me. It's an order from the Commander, and we are bound to obey," told the soldier.

"He is my father, and I won't come without him. You can go, but I am not coming, soldier." Littpin made her stand clear.

The silence broke, and a heavy wind blew there, precisely the same as the one that made the fire extinguish earlier.

The remaining soldiers and the Captain surveyed the area around the bushes while Venkad and Muthu gazed upwards at the sky, seemingly anticipating the arrival of a colossal creature.

The Captain surmised that Venkad and Muthu were searching for a larger snake, and his intuition proved to be correct. Before long, a massive snake with two heads appeared before them, one resembling that of a python and the other a cobra. The cobra head had red eyes, while the python's eyes were green. Its black scales were noticeably tougher than those of the other snakes they had encountered.

"King Cobrython," Venkad and Muthu exclaimed in unison.

Chapter 24
THE REVENGE OF COBRYTHON

The soldiers were terrified when they saw Cobrython, and they immediately took cover behind Venkad and Muthu.

They thought to themselves,

"This is the end."

Littpin was gripped with panic as she lay on the ground, but she quickly rose to her feet, grabbed her sword, and ran towards Venkad. This left the Captain in awe as he watched the injured Littpin sprinting towards her father. Even the soldiers of Vaani Sena were taken aback and stepped back upon seeing the creature crawling towards them. Littpin, however, ran straight towards her father, who was standing courageously facing the Cobrython.

Littpin grabbed her father and said,

"Father, let's go from here, please...."

Venkad held her hands and told her to remain calm.

And he sheathed his swords and advanced a few steps towards Cobrython.

Littpin, the soldiers and the Captain were appalled, and the Captain asked Muthu,

"What is the Commander doing?

Are we going to surrender?"

Muthu didn't dare to utter a word and remained silent.

After a period of silence, the Cobrython began to stir, its two heads hissing and shifting.

"Is the beast talking to the commander?"

"Can the commander speak with the beast?"

"What are they speaking?"

"How could the Commander speak with this beast? Does he know their language?"

The Captain was left perplexed by such thoughts.

Littpin seeing this, asked Muthu,

"Uncle, did father know this Snake?"

Muthu signalled Littpin to remain silent, but she didn't heed his signal and continued.

"Uncle, please...tell me who this Snake is and how does father know it? Does this Snake have any kind of enmity towards him? Tell me, something uncle..." asked Littpin with a shivering voice.

"Littpin, please remain calm. If you shout, you will draw Cobrython's attention towards you." Said Muthu in a soft tone.

Littpin raised her sword and said

"Uncle, we should draw the beast's attention away from my father. He is in danger."

"No, no...Littpin put down your sword," shouted Muthu.

Hearing Muthu's voice, Venkad looked back and saw Littpin with a raised sword ready to charge king Cobrython.

"Oh, my dear", whispered Venkad.

Littpin charged towards Cobrython with the war cry, "Sarparna Sthabdh."

The Captain and soldiers were amazed by seeing Littpin's courage, and they, too, followed the charging Littpin by shouting the war cry,

"Sarparna Sthabdh"

"Sarparna Sthabdh"

However, unlike the other snakes, King Cobrython was not deterred by this war cry, leading the Captain to conclude that this creature must be more powerful.

The Cobrython saw the charging soldiers and Littpin; he hissed loudly and blew strongly through his python head. The heavy wind from Cobrython's blew the charging team to the ground.

As Cobrython gazed at Venkad once more, he saw tears welling up in Venkad's eyes and observed him standing there in silence. Venkad had not anticipated the foolish actions of Littpin and the soldiers.

Undeterred, Littpin and the soldiers rose to their feet and once more advanced towards Cobrython with their war cry.

"Sarparna Sthabdh"

"Sarparna Sthabdh"

Despite witnessing the sheer power and size of Cobrython, Littpin and the soldiers did not lose hope and were determined to face the beast on the battlefield. Their hope for a chance to reunite with their loved ones drove them towards this courageous venture, even though they lacked confidence in their military skills to win against the mighty creature.

As King Cobrython charged towards them, Venkad delivered a sudden blow to its belly with his eagle pommel sword, causing the beast to hiss loudly in pain and look down at its stomach. Though there was no bleeding, Venkad realised that his sword had become blunt after melting its tip to save the General's horse at the lord's palace stables. After getting preoccupied, Venkad had forgotten to fix the blade, and now it was unable to cut through Cobrython's significantly sturdier scales.

However, even with a blunt sword, Venkad managed to make Cobrython suffer, proving that his power should not be underestimated.

Cobrython tried to strike Venkad with its fang, but he dodged. Venkad made his next move by striking the fang of Cobrython, and the sharp teeth fell on the ground. Blood oozed out of its mouth, and the battleground trembled with its loud hissing sound.

During that time, Venkad approached Muthu. and warned him,

"His revenge has started, and it is upon us."

"But we haven't done anything to attract his revenge, brother." Said Muthu.

"He believes that we burned their settlements and started this war." Said Venkad.

"Those three soldiers are the ones who started this fire, and he believes we sent them." Continued Venkad.

"Oh brother, what will we do now?" Asked Muthu.

"Muthu, you take Littpin and go to the lord's palace and tell the lord about everything that has happened here and ask him to report this to General Atheendra." Said Venkad.

"Brother, what about you? I am not leaving your side. If I am going, you will come with me." Told Muthu.

"Listen, Muthu, this is a direct order, and you must comply with it. Take the fallen teeth of Cobrython with you, as only then will the lord believe you. And don't forget to bring the Captain along; you'll need his assistance," commanded Venkad. He then turned towards the furious Cobrython.

As the beast slithered towards Venkad, it quickly coiled itself around him and began to squeeze him tightly. In a daring move, Littpin leaped towards Cobrython and swung her sword at its remaining tooth, which was poised to bite Venkad. With a loud scream, Cobrython lost its final tooth due to Littpin's strike, and it lost the grip on Venkad, causing him to tumble to the ground. Without hesitation, Littpin rushed towards her father and lifted him up.

"Father, let's go from here." Said Littpin.

"No, dear, I must stop him at any cost." Said Venkad. Muthu arrived at the battleground along with the Captain by that time.

"Littpin, let's go." Said Muthu.

"No, uncle, I can't leave father here." Said Littpin with a trembling tone.

"Take her, Muthu and leave now." Ordered Venkad.

Before they could do anything, the Cobrython struck them with its tail causing them to fall. When the soldiers on the battlefield attempted to attack the Cobrython, it delivered a powerful blow that killed them instantly. Venkad surveyed the aftermath of the battle and noticed that only five soldiers had survived. Helplessly he asked Muthu to leave before it's too late.

As the Cobrython attempted to strike Venkad with its tail, he managed to evade the attack. However, the Cobrython surprised Venkad with a reverse movement, causing him to fall and lose his grip on his sword. The weapon landed in front of Littpin, who was still lying on the ground, and upon seeing her father defenceless, she trembled with fear.

Even with squirming pain, she stood up and quickly ran to grab the sword. Soon after grabbing the sword Littpin looked up and realised that Venkad was no longer on the battlefield. She then witnessed the Cobrython devouring a large object that appeared to be Venkad's body. Littpin was overwhelmed with emotion, and she couldn't bring herself to speak or cry. She felt a sense of numbness in her hands, and tears flowed uncontrollably down her face. Despite her blurred vision, her gaze remained fixated on the spot where her father was last seen standing.

Despite the shock of her father's death, Littpin held onto his sword with a firm grip. She had begged Venkad to retreat from the battle, fearing that he would meet his demise at the hands of the giant Snake she had seen in her dreams. Sadly, her worst fears were realised, and she was left feeling utterly lost and alone.

The Captain quickly took charge of the situation and rushed Littpin towards the exit of the battlefield. They navigated a small rock tunnel that led to the outer forest, which the Cobrython was too large to follow. However, the Snake saw them attempting to escape and began to crawl swiftly towards them.

Suddenly, the Cobrython's vision became blurred as Muthu, and the remaining soldiers lit a fire on top of the cave tunnel using their weapons made of a special alloy and iron. The reflection of the fire persisted for a while, providing a window of opportunity for Muthu and the remaining soldiers to escape through the cave tunnel before the Cobrython regained its sight.

Chapter 25

THE PROUD BROTHER

Captain and Littpin were joined by the five soldiers and Muthu inside the tunnel. Littpin was sitting against the cave wall with her eyes downcast and was not looking at anyone. Muthu approached her and sat beside her, holding her tightly. Unexpectedly, it was Muthu who began crying loudly instead of Littpin.

Even though the Captain tried to lift him, Muthu was so heavy, not physically but emotionally, due to his deep connection with Venkad, who was more than a brother to him. Muthu was struggling to come to terms with the fact that his beloved brother had passed away.

With his head down on the ground, he whispered, "Brother, where are you?"

"Why did you leave me alone?"

"You were with me since I was born, and I have grown by looking at you. But how can I live without you, brother?"

And he continued crying.

The Captain and the five soldiers were overwhelmed by the emotions of Littpin and Muthu. Littpin seemed disheartened, and Muthu was grieving the loss of his brother. They all sat down on the ground, leaning against the rocky wall.

As the Captain closed his eyes, he was flooded with memories of Venkad - his first encounter, Venkad's motivational speeches to the soldiers, his affection towards his daughter, and his brave acts of killing snakes. Tears streamed down his face as he reminisced.

They spent the whole night inside the cave tunnel, with only a few small openings providing a glimpse of the outside world. The soldiers guarding the entrance informed the Captain that dawn had arrived as the sun's rays penetrated through these openings. The Captain stretched his body and nudged Muthu's shoulder to wake him up. Muthu looked at Littpin, who had her eyes half-closed, clutching Venkad's eagle pommel sword to her chest. The Captain was taken aback by Littpin's unusual sleeping position.

The Captain looked at Muthu,

"She might have heard mind voices, and that's why her eyes are like this. Nothing to worry about, Captain." Said Muthu.

Captain nodded in agreement and realised Muthu had not regained his strength completely. He tried to console Muthu and said

"Even though Commander is no longer physically present, he will always live on through you and Littpin. Venkad had trained you both, and every time you speak or fight, you embody his spirit. Whenever you feel defeated or low, Venkad also feels the same. Do you wish your brother to be defeated?"

"No, Captain, his head will always be high. And I will not let my brother down; He is my pride."

Said Muthu, with his head held high.

Chapter 26

LOST AND FOUND

Muthu gently tried to take the sword from Littpin, and she woke up suddenly,

"Father, I will..." she stopped abruptly, realising that her father is no more. She didn't shed tears, but her eyes turned red as she took deep breaths and remained silent once again.

The group embarked on their journey towards the outskirts of the forest, intending to report the incidents to Tamnat's lord. Muthu and the Captain engaged in a discussion about how to present the information to the lord and council, expressing concerns about whether they would believe their story.

Muthu suggested using the fallen fangs of Cobrython as evidence to convince them.

"If we show them the fangs, they will have no choice but to believe us," he said.

"Yes, they will believe it for sure." Said Captain looking at his leather bag within which the two fangs are kept.

They kept sauntering as swift movements would alert the enemies if they were anywhere on the pathway.

As they made their way, the group's lead soldier informed them that a body was visible ahead on their path. Upon hearing this, the Captain motioned for them all to stop. He then selected two soldiers to accompany him and investigate the body while Muthu and the remaining soldiers stayed put to guard Littpin.

They discovered that the body was that of a Vaani Sena soldier, which was strange since all of the soldiers from that army had died on the battlefield, except for the five soldiers currently with their group.

The Captain motioned for one of the soldiers to turn the body over and reveal the soldier's face, and to his surprise, it was one of the three missing soldiers from their group. Additionally, the Captain noticed traces of oil on the soldier's clothing and hand, which caused him to be even more alarmed.

"Oh no…" the Captain said.

"The commander already had doubts about them, but I believed them blindly."

"I should have watched the three soldiers with extra care."

"All these wouldn't have happened".

"What could be the reason behind setting fire to those settlements, and on whose order?"

"It must be a well-planned conspiracy."

"And what happened to the other two soldiers who disappeared with this one?"

Numerous frightening ideas flooded the Captain's mind, and he signalled to Muthu that it was safe to proceed. Muthu then approached them and said,

"Littpin and my brother already had suspicions regarding this soldier and his friends. He knows what happened. Wake him up, soldier." Ordered Muthu

The soldier disarmed the sleeping soldier as per the Captain's order. And tied both of his hands together.

The sleeping soldier started waking up amidst the fury of Littpin and Muthu.

Chapter 27
THE ROGUE SOLDIER

As his eyes slowly opened, he was jolted with shock to discover himself bound and encircled by the Captain and his crew. The Captain dealt a powerful blow to his face, causing his nose to bleed profusely, and as his hands were restrained, he was unable to stem the blood flow. The Captain glared at him with rage, but the soldier averted his gaze, prompting the Captain to strike him once more and repeat his words sternly.

"Bastard, look at me."

He glared at the Captain with anger. Not tolerating the soldier's defiance, the Captain delivered a forceful kick, causing the soldier to scream in agony. Concerned that the noise might attract the enemy, the Captain signalled for the guards to silence the soldier. Muthu advised the Captain to delay the interrogation and continue their journey, and the Captain agreed, instructing his men to bring the captive along as they proceeded towards the outskirts of the forest. Muthu then informed the Captain that two other soldiers were stationed at the forest's edge and needed rescuing.

And the Captain said,

"It was a grave mistake from my side not to post soldiers outside the deep forest. I was in a hurry when I heard the explosive sound and saw the fire, and I forgot to post the soldiers there."

Muthu pat on his shoulder and said,

"It is okay, Captain, and everyone makes mistakes at some point."

Captain smiled at Muthu, and they continued their journey. And he had many thoughts in his mind.

"Where are the other two rogue soldiers?"

"Are they dead? Maybe."

"Cobrython might have swallowed them."

One question suddenly striked through his mind.

"What was the explosive sound I heard when the forest fire started?"

And he thought,

"Muthu might know it".

"Muthu and the Commander already knew about the Cobrython also. So, he will know this also for sure."

He approached Muthu, separated him from the rest of the team, and posed the question.

"The fire set by the rogue soldiers exploded the snakes' eggs, and that is the reason why king Cobrython got furious and attacked us with full might", said Muthu.

"How do you know about that?" Asked Captain.

"There were broken eggshells all over the battleground." Said Muthu.

Captain realised what the broken white pieces were as he tried to recollect his memory.

He said,

"So, the war was a fair one…."

Muthu nodded his head and said,

"From both sides…."

Because it was the rogue soldiers who set ablaze the settlements and the egg and not the Vaani Sena. Nevertheless, for the outlaws and Cobrython, those soldiers were part of the Vaani Sena and didn't know they went rogue. So, the war seems fair from both ends.

Chapter 28
AND THEIR WATCH ENDS

As they neared the end of the cave tunnel, Muthu signalled to the Captain to stop. He advised the Captain to first inspect the tunnel's exit before proceeding outside, suspecting that an ambush may be waiting for them. Cobrython, who had spotted them entering the tunnel, may have stationed himself or his army of snakes at the tunnel's end to launch an attack.

To investigate the situation, the Captain instructed one soldier to venture forth and examine the tunnel's end and the surrounding area. The soldier stealthily made his way out of the tunnel and scanned the environment for any signs of activity, but the forest was peaceful and undisturbed. The soldier then proceeded to inspect the perimeters, as per Muthu's instruction, searching for any evidence of snake tracks on the ground.

After some time, the soldier came back and reported to the Captain,

"Captain, the road ahead is completely safe, and there are no signs of ambush".

"What about the crawl marks, soldier?" Asked Muthu.

"No crawl marks also." Replied the soldier.

The Captain looked at Muthu, waiting for his reply.

"Okay, Let's go." Said Muthu.

Littpin was physically present but completely oblivious to what was happening around her. After the team exited the cave tunnel, Muthu kept a watchful eye on their surroundings. He eventually declared, "It's safe to proceed. I don't see any indication of Cobrython or his snake army."

Muthu felt that something was odd.

"This is very odd. Cobrython must have found some way to reach here before us, but what happened?"

"His revenge will be complete only when he destroys us and the entire Vaani sena."

"But what happened to him?"

Muthu abruptly pushed aside these haunting thoughts and urged the team to move quickly. Memories of Venkad's gruesome demise at the hands of Cobrython flooded Muthu's mind, and the images of the last moments of Venkad's life were particularly distressing. Littpin had only witnessed the sight of Venkad's body disappearing down the serpent's gullet, but Muthu had seen the entire ordeal unfold before his eyes. The incident would forever haunt him, and he couldn't shake off the chilling memory from his mind.

After a tiring journey, they reached the forest outposts at the edge of the deep forests where the two soldiers were posted by Venkad for the watch.

Muthu's suspicions were aroused, prompting him to signal the team to halt and seek cover in the nearby bushes. Muthu and the Captain, however, decided to climb a nearby tree to get a better view of their surroundings.

From their vantage point, they observed some unusual movements emerging from the depths of the forest, heading towards the border outposts. Their presence heightened the sense of danger, and Muthu and the Captain knew they had to be cautious and remain vigilant.

"It's Vaani Sena."

Said the Captain, and he started climbing down nevertheless Muthu stopped him and asked him to remain in the tree.

The Captain was perplexed by Muthu's decision to stop and hide, as he believed the approaching movement was likely to be the Vaani Sena reinforcements.

Captain said, "But Muthu...."

Muthu closed Captain's mouth with his hand and signalled him to remain quiet. He asked the Captain to look inside the bushes near the outposts, where the two soldiers were posted by Venkad. The Captain was taken aback to find the two soldiers still inside the bush.

"So, these are not the reinforcements?" Asked the Captain quietly.

Muthu nodded his head and said, "No, they are not."

"If it was reinforcements called by these two soldiers, then they would have joined the reinforcement team when they entered the deep forest through the outposts." the Captain thought.

"So, the reinforcement teams had not entered through the boundary outposts, and there is no other entry point also." The Captain stopped his breath for some time due to the shock, and he said,

"So, they are not the Vaani Sena."

"They are not the Vaani Sena. The outlaws took the Vaani Sena uniform from our soldier's bodies," said Muthu.

The Captain's eyes widened in shock, and he exclaimed, "So these enemy soldiers are pretending to be Vaani Sena troops? The two soldiers stationed there won't realise the danger until it's too late!"

The Captain suggested they warn the two soldiers, but Muthu quickly dismissed the idea

"No, Captain. We cannot do that. We cannot take a risk at this juncture," said Muthu; he continued,

"It is also important that we must be alive to report the incidents to the lord of Tamnat."

The Captain recognised Muthu's practicality and chose to remain a silent observer.

A group of outlaws disguised in Vaani Sena uniforms arrived at the bush where soldiers were stationed. Upon seeing the uniform, the soldiers felt relieved and emerged from their hiding spot. The outlaws, mistaking the soldiers for an ambush, quickly took up a defensive stance. However, they soon realised that it was only two soldiers on watch duty near the boundary.

The outlaws demanded the soldiers surrender, but the soldiers refused and raised their swords in challenge. Knowing they would likely suffer losses if they engaged in combat with the Vaani Sena soldiers, the outlaws hesitated. Suddenly, a massive iron net was dropped on the soldiers, trapping them and rendering their swords useless. The outlaws then took the soldiers as prisoners and retreated back into the forest, happy with their victory and anticipating their reward.

Despite the soldiers' defeat, the Captain was proud of their bravery and refusal to surrender even in the face of overwhelming odds.

Captain exclaimed with a deep breath,

"And now their watch ends."

Chapter 29
TO THE PALACE

After the two soldiers were captured by the outlaws, Muthu, Captain, Littpin, and the soldiers had no choice but to continue their journey toward the palace.

Muthu advised the Captain to question the rogue soldier outside the palace before presenting him to the court, to which the Captain responded by saying,

"I know a suitable location for the interrogation."

Muthu concurred. He said,

"Captain, you should be very careful because we don't know who our enemy is, and do not reveal this incident to anyone. If things are not going as our plan, please take Littpin to Malnat and meet a man named Dravas. If you need any assistance, he will be there to help you".

Agreeing to the plan, the Captain and his team arrived at the city center through a secret passage that only the Captain was aware of. To avoid attracting attention, they were all in disguise. Taking Littpin, the rogue soldier, with them, the Captain and his soldiers brought him to an underground cellar, where they secured him to a wooden chair and removed the cloth that had been keeping him quiet on the journey.

Littpin remained in the corner of the cellar, staring wearily at her father's eagle pommel sword, while the Captain instructed one of his soldiers to fetch food and water for both Littpin and the rest of the team. To ensure the soldier remained inconspicuous, the Captain cautioned him not to draw any attention while shopping in the city.

As the Captain sharpened his dagger, the rogue soldier realised that he would soon face interrogation by the Captain.

Muthu approached the palace gate and overheard the soldiers engaged in a deep discussion, catching snippets of words such as "rebellion," "usurper," and "treason." However, he couldn't quite discern the context of their conversation. When Muthu requested to see the lord of Tamnat, the soldiers searched him for weapons, confiscating his daggers before leading him to meet the lord.

As he made his way to the meeting, Muthu couldn't help but ponder:

"We have met with the lord on numerous occasions before, and our weapons were never confiscated like this."

And Muthu couldn't resist asking the escort soldiers; he asked.

"Soldier, why did you confiscate my weapons.? "I used to visit the lord with my weapons on me," Muthu commented, sensing that something was amiss.

"Times change," one of the soldiers retorted arrogantly. Despite his unease, Muthu continued to follow the escort soldiers to the lord of Tamnat's chambers.

Chapter 30
THE COMMANDER

Upon arriving at the palace, Muthu was granted entry into the courtroom by the guards. Surprisingly, the escort soldiers accompanying him were also allowed inside, which caused Muthu to have a sense of unease since this was not typical protocol.

He noticed that the lord of the Tamnat was already seated on his throne alongside the other chiefs. Sensing the gravity of the situation, Muthu suspected that the reason for the meeting might be related to him as well.

At the same time, the Captain was about to start the interrogation. He approached the rogue soldier, who was already prepared for the interrogation.

The Captain put his hands on the shoulders of the rogue and asked,

"You bastard, do you know what you have done?"

"Don't you know, Captain, what happened?" replied the rogue soldier.

The rogue soldier's arrogant demeanour angered the Captain to the point where he couldn't contain himself.

In response, he placed his boot on the soldier's foot and crushed his toe. Despite the soldier's screams, they were muffled by the fact that they were in an underground cellar.

"Now tell me, what have you done?" Asked the Captain.

Despite the Captain's attempts to extract information, the rogue soldier remained tight-lipped about the incident. Realising that he wasn't going to divulge anything, the Captain grew disheartened.

Just then, the soldier who had gone to fetch food and water knocked on the door three times, as per the pre-arranged signal agreed upon by the Captain. The door was opened, and the soldier entered the room, only to find the Captain standing despondently in the corner.

He went to the Captain and reported,

"Captain, rumours are spreading about the forest fire".

"What kind of rumours?" Asked the Captain.

The soldier looked at Littpin, who was devastated by her father's death. He came close to the Captain and whispered something in his ear.

The rogue soldier observed this exchange and noticed a sudden change in the Captain's demeanour - his eyes turned a fiery red, and he clenched his fists and jaw, causing the rogue soldier to feel intimidated.

Without hesitation, the Captain grabbed his sharpened dagger and swiftly moved towards the rogue soldier, cutting off his right fist. He then squeezed the severed portion and demanded,

"What was the plan?"

"We three have been asked to go to the settlements of the outlaws and set fire to it, which would start a rebellion from the outlaws." Replied the soldier, who was in extreme pain.

"What about the other two?" Asked the Captain.

"I didn't see them after the snakes attacked us, and most probably, the snakes would have killed them, and I managed to escape somehow", said the soldier.

"What was the motive?" Asked the Captain.

"To look like this was done by chief Venkad to usurp the lordship from the lord of Tamnat." said the rogue soldier.

Littpin was taken aback by the words of the rogue soldier. Despite her immense grief, she managed to stand up and approach the soldier, her voice quiet and low as she asked,

"Who gave the order?"

"Chief Marutha." Replied the rogue soldier.

All of a sudden, everyone in the room heard a sickening sound of blood splattering on the floor, followed by a loud thud. All eyes in the room turned to the rogue soldier.

The rogue soldier's body was filled with blood, and his head was rolling down on the floor.

The Captain and the soldiers turned their attention towards Littpin, who stood firmly on the ground with her father's eagle pommel sword pointed towards the floor. Her body was covered in blood, and she wiped the blood off her father's sword and said,

"Even his blood is stinking."

The Captain and soldiers were frightened to see Littpin in such a state. She appeared almost otherworldly like Goddess Gordha, with her fiery red eyes and bloodied sword in hand. In awe, the Captain fell to his knees before her and took out his dagger, cutting his palm in front of Littpin. He then said,

"Commander, from this moment onwards to the end of my life, I will follow your command."

The soldiers and the Captain were not in awe of Littpin solely because of her physical appearance, but rather they were impressed by her quick decision-making skills and immense bravery in executing justice.

By carrying out the execution of the rogue soldier, she provided closure and justice for all the soldiers who had lost their lives on the battlefield. Inspired by her leadership and bravery, the soldiers also followed her example by taking a blood oath to uphold justice and fight for their fallen comrades.

"Captain, we must go to the palace court. Uncle is in danger."

Said Littpin, the new Commander of the Captain and the five soldiers. And the Captain's eyes were downcast. And Littpin realised something had already happened.

"What was it, Captain?"
Littpin asked.

"Muthu was arrested at the palace court on the orders of the lord of Tamnat."

Littpin clenched her fists and looked at the Captain. He was not able to look into her eyes.

After her father's death in battle and her uncle's subsequent arrest and imprisonment, Littpin found herself an orphan. As she gazed upon her father's sword, she spoke quietly to herself:

"I will avenge you, father".

Her revenge was not just against the Cobrython but also against Chief Marutha, who plotted this evil plan to frame Venkad, a Usurper.

Chapter 31
TO MALNAT

"Captain, tonight we have to rescue uncle from the prison. Make all the arrangements", ordered Littpin.

The Captain disagreed with this order, and he opposed it,

"Commander, your uncle already gave directions to go to Malnat if things are not as planned. And now he is arrested, and we must go to Malnat and meet a man named Dravas."

"Dravas uncle?" Littpin asked.

"Yes, Commander, do you know him?" the Captain asked Littpin.

"I have heard of him but never saw him and don't know how he looks," Littpin replied.

She asked the Captain about the possibility of rescuing Muthu.

"Commander, your uncle is locked in Manchithra prison, which is heavily guarded by the Vaani Sena as well as wild dogs who are trained to detect smell even from a farther distance," said the Captain.

"So, what should we do, Captain?" Asked Littpin.

"We have only one way to find the solution to all our problems. We have to reach Malnat."

Littpin agreed to this plan hesitantly because her only remaining blood relative was now locked in prison, and she felt helpless to assist him. Nonetheless, they packed their belongings and cleaned up the bloodstains on the floor before burning the rogue soldier's body. The reason for this was that if the authorities discovered a beheaded Vaani Sena soldier in the city centre, who was already in Venkad's platoon, the lord of Tamnat would become infuriated and might even order a death sentence for Muthu.

Therefore, they set out on their journey towards Malnat, all of them disguised and without any armour or swords. Instead of swords, they carried daggers in their sheaths, while the swords were bundled in a cloth bag. Littpin carefully wrapped her father's sword in cloth and hid it among her clothing.

Littpin wished to see Veera, Sugandhi, and Virumen before they left for Malnat. But the Captain advised her to drop that plan,

"Commander, the spies, must have already deployed around your home since they don't know whether we are alive or dead, and the moment we reach home, they will arrest us."

Littpin understood how vigilant her Captain was, and she nodded her head, and they resumed their journey towards Malnat, a land of social prosperity.

She heard many stories about Malnat from her father. Malnat is known for its hospitality towards visitors from other regions and is free from discrimination. This is why Muthu suggested that Littpin should go to Malnat with the Captain.

Additionally, if the Vaani Sena wants to arrest them in Malnat, they would need the approval of both the Chief of Malnat and the General of the Bharatha Army. This means that the Vaani Sena would need General Atheendra's permission to capture Littpin, and he is likely to comprehend the scheme behind these events. Muthu understands this fact and specifically directs the Captain to take Littpin to Malnat.

On their journey to Malnat, Littpin's heart felt very heavy, and many memories flooded her mind- Her father, Muthu, Veera, their home, Sugandhi, and Virumen. Life at Tamnat was beautiful for her, with her father by her side and Muthu to support her whenever she did something naughty. But now everything has changed. Littpin no longer remained that carefree, playful girl.

Her mind is now consumed by a single desire - revenge and nothing else occupies her thoughts.

Chapter 32
THE CLIMB

Tamnat and Malnat are adjacent provinces, and they share the same land boundaries. Due to the presence of Vaani Sena checking passengers along the border, Littpin and the team cannot cross the border without getting arrested. Therefore, the Captain informed Littpin,

"Commander, we cannot go through the boundary, and we have to go through the forest and climb the rock hill to reach Malnat."

"The Rockhill? but that is very difficult to climb." Said Littpin.

"Yes, Commander, but we have got no other option," said Captain.

"But Captain, there is another problem; Cobrython and his army of snakes might be inside the forest as well," Littpin said.

"Yes, we must travel as quickly as possible inside the forest, as this is our only option," Captain replied.

Despite the presence of Cobrython and his army of snakes, she did not fear them. However, she needed time to prepare for the upcoming war with Cobrython. Her father's eagle pommel sword was blunt and needed fixing, and she also required more warriors to join her in the fight.

As they travelled through the forest, they moved quickly and cautiously. Suddenly, they heard some rustling noises, prompting Littpin to order her team to stop and form a defensive formation. They observed the movements in the bushes, waiting for the enemy to attack first since they were outnumbered. As they watched carefully, two people came out of the bushes. Seeing them, Captain looked at Littpin with relief.

It was a boy, and a girl in their teens, and they were shocked to see armed people in front of them. Observing their unkempt appearance, the Captain murmured to Littpin,

"They must be mountain shepherds."

"Please spare our lives, we have nothing of value," pleaded the boy in distress, mistaking Littpin and the team for a gang of robbers.

The Captain inquired, "Do you tend to sheep, young man?"

The boy grew more fearful and replied, "Please don't take our sheep. They are our only means of survival, and we will die without them," he implored.

"What is your name?" Asked Littpin.

"Akshuru," said the boy.

"And what about you?" Littpin asked the girl whose eyes were fixed on the ground.

"Kripuya," the girl said in a lowered voice.

"Okay. Listen, we do not want your gold or sheep. But you need to help us climb the Rockhill. Also, gather your friends." Said Littpin.

The boy nodded his head, and he said,

"Okay, lady. I don't have any friends here; all the other members are elders, but I can help you. Let me take the climbing tools, and I will join you."

Littpin had a sense of trust towards the boy and girl, and so she permitted them to return to their settlement unharmed. Having learned from her father about the mountain shepherds and their habits, Littpin allowed the boy to retrieve their tools and return.

This incident validated what the Captain had told Muthu in the cave tunnel. Though Venkad was no longer alive, his words had a lasting impact, and they had instilled a sense of trust in Littpin towards the shepherd boy. Venkad's legacy lived on through Littpin's actions.

The Captain asked,

"Can we trust them?"

"Yes, he will join us as soon as we reach the bottom of the Rockhill," Littpin said.

And they resumed their journey toward the Rockhill.

The soldiers were talking to themselves about the incident on their way to the Rockhill

Soldier: "Do we look like thugs?"

And the Captain who overheard this said,

"Definitely. Now we do look like them."

The soldiers erupted in laughter, and Littpin joined in with a smile. She understood that it was crucial for the Captain to maintain the morale of his troops, and occasional moments of entertainment could help alleviate the stress of warfare.

They arrived at the base of the Rockhill and waited patiently for the shepherd boy to return.

"Will the boy come?" asked the Captain.

"He will come," Littpin said.

And before they could speak another word, the boy came riding a mule with two bags on both sides of the mule.

He unpacked all the tools, approached Littpin, and said,

"My lady, I have bought all the tools for us to climb the hill."

"Then what are we waiting for? Let's start ". The Captain said before Littpin could say anything.

Littpin nodded, and they all started climbing the Rockhill with the help of the shepherd boy.

Chapter 33

THE COOL BREEZE

Following a strenuous climb, they finally made it to the summit of the Rockhill. Littpin took a deep breath and sat down to rest. The temperature was notably colder at the top, and everyone began shivering. However, the shepherd boy had anticipated this and had brought blankets for them all to use.

The Captain felt remorse for not trusting the boy earlier; he hugged him tightly and said,

"You are a good lad."

The boy just smiled and didn't say anything. Littpin came to the boy and said,

"Thank you, Akshuru. You did a great help. What can I do for you?"

"Thank you, My lady. I don't want anything, and I am happy that I could help you."

Littpin smiled as Akshuru bid farewell to them and began his descent down the Rockhill. As they watched him climb down, the Captain remarked, "We owe him a great deal, Commander."

Littpin nodded in agreement and replied, "Absolutely, Captain. Without Akshuru's help, this climb would have been much more difficult, if not impossible."

The Captain said,

"Yes, Commander, that is true. Even though I said we could climb this Rockhill, I was not sure how we could do it."

"It was your unwavering hope, Captain, that led us to the top of this Rockhill," Littpin remarked with a sense of pride. She was grateful to have the best Captain to lead their army against the Cobrython and Marutha.

Littpin reflected on the power of hope, which gave people a reason to keep going despite difficult circumstances. It instilled immense courage in individuals to fight against the odds and illuminated the darkest moments of life with a new light. She recalled her father's words about hope, which had helped her to move forward even after the death of her mother, Bhuvina.

As she gazed at the Captain and their soldiers enjoying the refreshing breeze, Littpin felt grateful for their shared hope and optimism for the future.

She called the Captain and said,

"Captain, let's move."

"Yes, Commander, we must reach there before night, and we have to find Dravas also."

They started their journey towards the city center of Malnat. And as they journeyed through the valleys of Rockhill, a booming voice echoed through the rocks, startling them all, and a soldier asked,

"What was it, Captain?"

"It must be some bird, probably an eagle calling for its mate." Said the Captain.

"But Captain, it's a loud voice." Said another soldier.

"Then the bird must also be huge", the Captain replied.

All of them started laughing, hearing this sarcastic reply from their Captain, and resumed their journey.

Chapter 34
THE BEAUTIFUL CAPITAL CITY

As they arrived at the City Centre, the Captain's eyes lit up with excitement, and he exclaimed, "Trivanat, the Capital city!"

Littpin couldn't help but admire the stunning city, but she quickly reminded herself of their mission. She turned to the Captain and asked,

"Captain, where can we find a weapon workshop in the city?"

And the Captain laughed and said,

"Commander, please have a look around the city."

As Littpin surveyed the city, she realised that most of the workshops were focused solely on weapon manufacturing. She was surprised by the sheer number of workshops dedicated to crafting weapons. She also remembered what her father had told her about the land of Malnat having some of the best weapon experts in the country.

The Captain said,

"Commander, I know a place where we can stay today, and it's almost getting late, and we may not be able to find Dravas today."

"Okay, Captain. But I need to fix the sword first," said Littpin.

The Captain assured Littpin that there was no immediate need for a sword as the Anantha Sena, known for their strength and efficiency, were in charge of the city's defence. Littpin agreed, having heard tales of the Anantha Sena from her father, and they made their way to the location the Captain had mentioned.

It was a sizable settlement situated outside the city center, home to many weapon traders, manufacturers, and suppliers. Although not a permanent settlement, it was well guarded by the Anantha Sena, who had set up flame throwers to deter any potential attacks.

Lord Manikta of Malnat was a staunch advocate of the safety and well-being of his people. He always ensured that no blood was shed on his land and stood for peace. However, he was not averse to using violence when necessary to maintain peace. Lord Manikta was known for his intelligence and shrewdness, and it was impossible to manipulate him.

After arriving at the settlement, the Captain entered their names in the registry with false information to maintain a low profile. They were provided with small but clean and well-kept rooms for the night.

Littpin kept her sword, wrapped in a cloth, under her bed. And she slowly slipped into a deep sleep as the journey was exhaustive.

The Captain instructed the soldiers to remain vigilant and take turns keeping watch. He specifically cautioned them to keep an eye on Littpin, as he suspected she might try to leave to repair her sword. The Captain knew that seeking revenge could weaken even the strongest person, and fighting with a vengeful mindset could lead to unnecessary bloodshed.

The Captain looked at Littpin, took a deep breath, and went to bed.

Chapter 35

THE RECRUITMENT

Littpin and the Captain began their search for Dravas early in the morning. They left one soldier behind at the settlement and assigned the other four to gather intelligence about the happenings in Tamnat after they left. Walking through the alleys, they entered a weapon workshop and began inspecting the weapons, looking for the specific alloy that Venkad and Muthu used to create weapons for battling the snakes.

Suddenly, they heard a commotion outside and inquired with the workshop owner. He informed them that an army recruitment was underway on the ground nearby. Curious, the Captain and Littpin made their way to the recruitment site, where a large crowd had already gathered to watch the proceedings. The Anantha Sena recruitment involved multiple tasks for the candidates.

The first task involves a wooden dummy, and candidates must showcase their hand-to-hand combat skills by striking it. The second task requires striking a hanging metal ball, which will move forward upon impact, and then the candidate must avoid being hit by the ball upon its return swing. The final task involves jumping over a six-foot barrier. Only those who pass all three stages will be selected for the Anantha Sena.

Littpin and the Captain watched the recruitment process with great interest, amazed by the candidates' performances. Four candidates had already passed the tests, and now the fifth candidate was up. He was a boy with a shaved head, and he did not appear to have a strong build. The boy is stout, and the In charge of the recruitment made a rude remark, asking loudly,

"Here comes the fatty. Are you able to complete even the first step?"

And the crowd burst into a laugh, and everyone started mocking him.

"Fatso, get out of the ground and find something to eat."

"Watch your belly, boy; it will fall."

"Don't shake the ground fatty."

Littpin got angry by hearing these, and she advanced, but the Captain grabbed her hand and requested to keep a low profile. Littpin realised that she needed to stay focused on her goal and not get emotional about every injustice she witnessed. However, she also spoke up, saying,

"This is very unfair, Captain. He had the courage and confidence to come and compete in the recruitment, but nobody has accepted it."

And the Captain said,

"Look at the boy, Commander. Does he seem to look sad or angry?"

Littpin closely watched the boy, and she was surprised to see that the boy was keeping his head high despite all the mockery. He was very much confident, and the crowd couldn't dispirit him.

"Bravo," she said.

The bell was rung, and the first step started. The boy bowed on the ground in a show of respect. And he reached the wooden dummy.

As he punched the wooden dummy, the crowd jeered at him once again for the lack of noise produced by his punches, unlike the earlier candidates who had made a loud sound. However, the Captain understood what was happening. With each punch, the wooden dummy developed several cracks, and the base on which it was fixed started shaking. No one other than the Captain noticed this, not even Littpin. The Captain's military experience was more than her age, and so was his observation capacity. Despite the mockery, the recruitment in charge gave the boy the green signal to proceed to the next stage as he showed some unique movements different from others.

As he entered the second stage, the crowd started laughing when they saw that he had a wooden sword instead of an iron one like the previous candidates. The second stage was already challenging for those who came with iron swords, so how would this boy be able to strike the heavy iron ball and make it move forward? This was the question on everyone's mind.

Even Littpin asked the Captain,

"Captain, what is this boy doing? How can he win this stage by using a wooden sword?"

And the Captain replied,

"Talent and intelligence ".

Littpin got shocked by hearing Captain's comment about the boy. Littpin also saw tears in Captain's eyes when he replied.

The Captain was pleased and satisfied by seeing the talent and intelligence of the boy.

He used a wooden sword because striking the metal ball with another metal would create intense vibrations inside the ball, which would cause jerking movements in the ball and the sword. These jerking motions will affect his next move when he has to strike the retreating ball. He has already done his calculations.

He passed the second stage and entered the third stage, in which he had to jump over a six-foot barrier.

The Captain knew that the boy would struggle with the third stage to clear a six-foot barrier with a tummy.

Despite this, the Captain still held hope that the boy would succeed in the final stage. When the bell for the third stage rang, the boy positioned himself at the starting line and prepared to run toward the barrier. The bell rang again, and he sprinted towards the barrier and attempted to jump over it. However, he collided with the top of the barrier and fell to the ground, causing the crowd to laugh once again.

The recruitment in charge approached the boy and helped him to stand up.

He stood up, smiled at the laughing crowds, and bowed to the crowd in a show of respect towards them. The crowd stopped laughing after seeing his pleasing gesture.

The recruitment In charge told the boy,

"Boy, you did a great job, and I will be very happy to take you into the Anantha Sena. But I am tied by rules; since you couldn't make the third round, I can't select you for the army."

The boy smiled, and he said,

"Thank you for the opportunity sir." He bowed and left the ground.

The Captain and Littpin too left the ground and they followed the boy.

Chapter 36
ABHEERA

The boy had a suspicion that he was being followed, so he opted to take a left turn into an alley instead of continuing straight. This left turn would lead to a dead end, which would confirm if the person following him was still pursuing him.

Littpin and the Captain also followed the same path and soon realised that it was a dead end. However, their relief was short-lived as the Captain suddenly felt something metallic against his neck. The boy had seized the Captain and held a dagger to his throat.

"Who are you?" Asked the boy.

"Easy boy, we are not your enemies; lower the weapon." Said, Captain.

Littpin swiftly unsheathed her concealed dagger with the red stone and demanded that the boy drop his weapon. The boy was momentarily stunned by the sight of the dagger, giving the Captain an opportunity to push him back with a headbutt. The boy winced in pain and rubbed his nose where it had been struck.

After regaining his composure, the boy sheathed his dagger and inquired once more, "Who are you, and why are you following me?"

"We have come to appreciate you," said the Captain.

Littpin complimented, "You performed exceptionally well during the selection process."

"It doesn't matter; I am not selected." The boy said.

"You have got the chance to participate in the selection process, and you successfully cleared the first two stages. Therefore, you should feel pleased about your achievement, and if you practice more, you can attend the selection process again.". Said Littpin.

"See, I haven't got selected, and that's what matters. You can say all these words to console me. But do you think these words could offer solace to a person who failed.?" Asked the boy.

The Captain realised that the boy was irritated, and there was no use in advising or motivating him further. So he changed the subject.

"What is your name, boy?"

"Abheera", said the boy.

"And what is your name?" Asked the boy.

The Captain was taken aback by the question since neither Littpin nor Muthu knew his name. They had all been referring to him as "Captain" since the beginning, so they had never bothered to ask his name.

The Captain replied, "It's Sajeera."

Abheera noted that their names had a similar sound

"Our names have a similar tone, Uncle." Said Abheera.

Littpin looked at the Captain when Abheera called him uncle, but he winked at Abheera, indicating that they needed to maintain a low profile.

Abheera didn't ask for Littpin's name, and she realised that he might be too reserved to talk to girls.

And the Captain said,

"That is it, Abheera; we just came to appreciate you and will see you again."

"Okay, Uncle, I will see you again, and next time, you can come directly to me; no need to follow around." Said Abheera with a wink.

And they parted and went to attend to their business.

Chapter 37
THE OUTLAW SPIES

That evening, they convened, and the soldiers informed them that the information from Tamnat hadn't yet arrived in Malnat. However, they received an alarming update that the Anantha Sena had discovered and eliminated two unauthorised entries at the border. Upon examining the deceased individuals, they discovered poisoned daggers in their possession.

"So, the Cobrython has started tracking us." The Captain said.

"But how do they know that we are here?" Littpin asked.

"They don't know we are here. Cobrython is sending outlaws to all the provinces to search for us". Captain replied.

"Captain, does Cobrython think these outlaws could overpower us?" Asked Littpin.

"No, Commander. These outlaws were just spying, and once they locate us, he will send his snakes to confirm the location, and once that is confirmed, he will attack with full might." Captain said.

"How do you know all this?" Asked the curious Commander.

"These are the protocols every Military follows to locate and kill someone," Captain said.

"Since the outlaws send to Malnat are dead, the Cobrython will send outlaws again, am I right, captain?" Asked Littpin.

"Yes, Commander. He will send outlaws again, and we should be cautious." Told the captain

"Captain, we have to find Dravas uncle by tomorrow itself. We cannot delay it anymore." Littpin said.

"Commander, we will start searching for Dravas tomorrow itself," Captain replied.

Littpin nodded and retired to her bed. She inspected the sword to ensure it was undamaged and proceeded to draw it out, planting a kiss on the blade, she said,

"I miss you, father".

She kept the sword under her bed and tried to sleep. But her mind was disturbed, and it was Abheera. Littpin couldn't shake off the words he had spoken to her regarding his failure to be selected.

"He may be feeling down, but his mindset towards failure isn't healthy,"

"He will require additional training and weight loss to overcome that obstacle."

"In any case, let's wait and see what's in store for him."

"Tomorrow, I must rise early to meet Drava's uncle as soon as possible."

"I also need to mend my sword."

"What can I do to assist Uncle Muthu?"

Numerous thoughts like these kept Littpin up that night, making it difficult for her to fall asleep.

Chapter 38
THE REUNION

Early morning, the Captain and Littpin woke up and began searching for Dravas. The soldiers were also instructed to search for Dravas, but they were assigned different directions to cover. As Littpin and the Captain arrived at the City Center during their search, they spotted Abheera walking ahead of them.

"Abheera..." called Captain.

Upon seeing the Captain and Littpin approaching, Abheera turned around and waited for them to catch up.

"Uncle, here again, today?" he inquired.

"Ha ha ha." Laughed Captain and said,

"Today, you were just ahead of us, and we weren't following."

Abheera chuckled at the remark, and his gaze fixated on Littpin's hand. Although the sword was wrapped in cloth, Abheera noticed the eagle-shaped pommel.

"Is that a sword," Abheera asked.

Littpin suddenly covered the pommel also and thought how careless she was. She didn't utter a word.

Abheera asked,

"Can I see that, please?" Abheera was a weapon enthusiast.

The Captain interrupted and said,

"Abheera, that sword is useless now, and we are searching for a weapon smith."

The Captain made the comment to divert Abheera's attention away from the sword. Little did he know, Abheera had a deep interest in weapons.

"I have extensive knowledge on how to repair and design swords. I can work on any sword," Abheera stated proudly.

While Littpin wanted to avoid Abheera's questions to protect their identities, she also knew she needed to repair the sword before any danger came their way.

"Can you do the work quickly?" Asked Littpin.

"Yes, I can guarantee that. I may have failed recruitment, but I am a weapon expert, and you can trust me." Said Abheera.

The three of them arrived at Abheera's home to fix Littpin's sword. Abheera brought the sword into his workshop and instructed them to rest while he worked on it. While the Captain looked around the home, he noticed that Abheera might not be living alone since there were other clothes present that may belong to an older adult.

Suddenly, Abheera emerged from the workshop with a shocked face and gestured for Littpin to follow him. They entered a dimly lit room with a fire altar at its centre and a table with a lamp in the corner. As Littpin looked at the table, she noticed her sword resting on it along with a distinctive helmet. A man behind the table called out to her, "Littpin."

Littpin was taken aback as a stranger called out her name in a place she had never visited before. Her mind went blank as she looked at Abheera, who was watching the man slowly approach her. As the man came into view, Littpin noticed that he was almost as tall as Abheera but had a slim build and patchy hair on his head, which was unusual since most people in Bharatha either had long hair or shaved heads.

The man stood in front of her and examined her face and eyes before saying,

"Your eyes are just like your mother's."

"Dravas uncle?" Asked Littpin.

"Yes, my dear." Replied the stranger.

Overwhelmed with emotion, Littpin embraced Dravas, her uncle, and began to cry uncontrollably. This was the first time she had cried so deeply since her father's death. Dravas had already suspected that something terrible had happened, as Littpin wouldn't have come to Malnat alone with the blunt sword of Venkad.

"Uncle, Father is dead," said Littpin.

Dravas was left stunned upon learning of his long-time friend's passing. Overwhelmed by the news, he lost all his strength and collapsed. Abheera and Littpin quickly came to his aid, helping him to a nearby bed in a separate room. The Captain, alerted by the sound of Dravas falling, rushed to the scene.

Dravas remained silent, unable to find the words to express his grief. Sensing his need for rest, Abheera asked Littpin to step outside with him.

"Father needs to rest, Littpin. The news was a shock to him, and it hit me hard as well," Abheera sympathised.

"Do you know my father?" Littpin inquired through her tears.

"Yes, my father always spoke highly of Venkad uncle. He was a great warrior and someone I deeply admire," Abheera replied, giving Littpin a sense of pride in her father.

As Littpin struggled to come to terms with her loss, Abheera offered her comfort and support.

"Littpin, your father is a great man, and great men never die. They live through their people."

Littpin was comforted by these words, and she smiled at Abheera.

Seeing this, the Captain thought to himself,

"How did Abheera manage to put her at ease so effortlessly? He has quite the charm."

Later on, Littpin and the Captain opted to spend the night at Dravas's residence with the intention of discussing their strategy with him.

Chapter 39
THE RESCUE

It was early morning, and the two soldiers found themselves bound and confined within a wooden prison. Through the cracks, they observed outlaws rushing about, blacksmiths forging weapons, and even witnessed playful newborn cobras frolicking amongst the foliage.

"They are preparing for a war," said one soldier.

"Yes, I can see that. But against whom?"

"Against Littpin"

"How do you know that?"

"I overheard some of the outlaws speaking."

"What you heard?"

"They have located Littpin and have sent the snakes to confirm it, and the snakes will kill Littpin if they get a chance."

"Oh. But where is Littpin now?"

"They themselves are uncertain about it. That's why they dispatched snakes to two different locations."

"Perhaps she is on the move, which is why they chose two locations."

"Maybe."

Their dialogue came to an abrupt halt as they heard rustling sounds coming from outside their cell. Initially, they assumed it was the little snakes playing about. To their surprise, they discovered a hole in the dungeon's flooring, from which an outlaw emerged and spoke in a hushed tone.

"Come with me." Said the outlaw.

"Who are you?" Asked both the soldiers together.

"I came to rescue you, idiots, can't you see it? Don't waste time, and come with me." Said the outlaw.

Placing their faith in him, the two soldiers fled their confinement through the hole the outlaws had created on the wooden floor. They trailed the outlaw to the forest's edge, where they discovered a woman and two other individuals waiting. The woman was outfitted in a body armour that dwarfed her size.

The soldiers were shocked to see one of the people standing along with the lady. His hands and legs were tied with an iron chain, and his mouth was gagged with a cloth. The other individual appeared to be a bodyguard charged with the woman's protection, sporting a high-quality dagger on his hip.

They approached the lady, and she asked the soldiers, pointing at the person who was in chains

"Do you know who this is?"

"Yes. He is our soldier who went missing on that day when all of this started." Said a soldier.

"You have to rephrase the sentence, soldier. He is the rogue soldier who has started all this menace." Said the lady.

The soldiers were taken aback upon learning of the treachery of the rogue soldier. The woman proceeded to divulge details regarding Muthu's arrest and Marutha's treachery, leaving the soldiers feeling deeply wounded. She implored them to take the rogue soldier into custody and have him confess before Lord Rakarna and other leaders.

The soldiers commenced their journey toward the City Center while the woman and her troops ventured further into the forest.

Chapter 40

AMMU

Littpin and the Captain woke up late as both could peacefully sleep at Dravas's home.

After freshening up, they sought out Dravas and found him in his workshop, diligently working on Littpin's eagle pommel sword.

"Come, Littpin. I was working on Venkad's sword." Said Dravas.

He continued,

"I am sorry we couldn't meet yesterday." Dravas apologised to the Captain.

"It's okay, Dravas. I can understand your situation. I have passed through the same situation after the Commander's death." Said Captain and introduced himself.

"Captain, it is not easy for me to forget the loss. But Venkad's death cannot go unpunished." Said Dravas.

"Uncle, can we fix the sword?" Asked Littpin.

"We have an issue dear, I don't have the alloy to fix the molten part at the tip, but I can surely make the sword sharp again," Dravas said.

"That will suffice, uncle; if the sword wasn't damaged, father might not have died," Littpin said.

"Dear, it was not the sword that made Venkad stronger. This sword was stronger only because it was Venkad who wielded it." Dravas said.

"Yes, Dravas. Whatever you said is damn true." Captain said.

"Where is Abheera, uncle?" Littpin asked.

"He went to the Rockhill to feed Ammu." Said Dravas.

"Ammu?" Asked Littpin.

"Oh, you didn't meet Ammu, right?" Dravas said.

"No, uncle," said Littpin.

Dravas instructed Littpin and the Captain to ready themselves for their journey to Rockhill, and they set out in the afternoon. Upon arriving at the valley near Rockhill, they spotted Abheera, who was clutching a massive chain and gazing skyward. As they drew nearer, Abheera turned towards the sound of footsteps and recognised the trio.

Dravas asked,

"Abhi, where is she?"

"She went hunting, father." Replied Abheera.

"What? I instructed you to ensure that she didn't roam outside. Why didn't you heed my words?" Dravas fumed, his face reddening with anger.

"Father, she deserves to be free at times, and she shouldn't be forced to live in chains," Abheera retorted, his face also contorted with fury as he flung the chains aside.

Dravas's ire continued to escalate upon witnessing his son's defiance, and he began to retort, "What do you mean by--"

Littpin interrupted Dravas and said,

"Uncle, please be calm; let's not argue here."

In a moment of realisation, he believed that Venkad was communicating with them through Littpin. He took a deep breath and listened to his friend's daughter's words.

Abheera turned to Littpin, offering her a grateful smile for her assistance in avoiding his father's wrath. Littpin returned the gesture with a sardonic nod.

Suddenly, the sound of flapping wings echoed throughout the valley, and a massive eagle, as large as Venkad himself, descended upon the group, landing beside Abheera. Abheera lovingly stroked the eagle's feathers and kissed its head, prompting the bird to raise its left wing and draw Abheera closer to its side.

"Ammu,..." called Dravas.

Dravas also greeted the eagle, stroking her feathers gently. Littpin and the Captain stared in amazement at the colossal bird, as they had never before seen an eagle of such a size. While they had encountered small birds such as ravens and palm-sized eagles before, the eagle before them was almost as large as Venkad himself. They stood there, awestruck, taking in the incredible sight before them.

"Ammu, see, we got guests." Dravas pointed towards Littpin and Captain.

Littpin approached Ammu with caution, trying not to show her fear. As she met the eagle's gaze, Littpin could feel her heart racing in her chest. However, to her surprise, Ammu slowly walked towards her and locked her eyes with Littpin's. With trembling hands, Littpin reached out to stroke Ammu's feathers. To her amazement, Ammu closed her eyes, seemingly at peace with Littpin's touch.

Abheera was shocked to see this, but Dravas looked calm and said,

"She liked Littpin."

And the Captain said,

"Yes. She is so friendly."

As the Captain reached out to touch Ammu's neck, she suddenly screeched and lunged at him. Abheera moved swiftly to restrain her. The Captain was taken aback by the sudden aggression and fell silent for a few moments, seeing him Dravas said,

"Ammu doesn't let any stranger near her; if anybody does, she will attack them."

"And that is why you put her in chains?" Asked Littpin.

"No, dear. No one in Bharatha country might have seen an eagle of this size, and if they find it, they will take her and summon her to King Vasaraya," said Dravas.

Littpin took a deep breath and replied,

"I understand, Uncle. Losing a beloved companion is always hard."

Her heart was heavy with the thought of Veera, unsure if he was alive or dead. She also felt guilty about leaving Virumen and Sugandhi behind when she escaped on the Flyer.

"Dear, where is the Flyer? Venkad might have given that to you on your seventeenth birthday, right?" Dravas asked Littpin.

"Yes, uncle. Father told me that it was you who gave him the Flyer. But I crash-landed it during the first battle."

After Dravas mentioned that the gift was mutual, Littpin became curious and asked,

"What was it, uncle? Please tell me?"

Dravas replied, "That story I will tell you later."

Just then, the Captain, who had been quiet for some time, regained his composure and asked,

"Shall we go home, Dravas?"

And everyone started laughing.

Dravas instructed Abheera to chain Ammu and place her in a hidden cage to avoid being seen. As they began their journey back home, it was already evening. Abheera, who was initially surprised by Ammu's affection towards Littpin, now understood the reason behind it and smiled at the thought. Littpin noticed his smile and asked about it, but he remained quiet.

On their way back, Abheera heard some noise, and he said,

"Father, there is something in the Rockhill".

"Come on, Abheera, there is nothing," Dravas replied irritably.

"Why, father? Why do you always ignore me? You never consider my words seriously. Why is it so? Asked Abheera.

Littpin realised that another fight would happen between the father and the son. She interrupted and said,

"Abheera, there is nothing here. Even if something is there, we are a group of four warriors who can manage it." Littpin tried to calm Abheera.

Abheera became irritated, and he said,

"No one believes my instincts and observations."

Littpin smiled at him and said,

"It is not like that, Abhi; we believe in you. You are a hero, and I have seen your performance on the ground that day." Littpin comforted him.

Abheera remained silent and looked around to investigate the noise he heard.

Littpin noticed Abheera surveying the surroundings and approached him, saying,

"Let's go home; there's nothing here."

Abheera nodded in agreement and walked ahead.

Littpin sensed that Abheera was still upset and tried to cheer him up, saying,

"If you're a good boy, you'll smile now."

This made Abheera laugh, and he admired Littpin's ability to comfort him. And he said,

"I will tell you a secret."

"What is it, Abhi?" Asked Littpin with curiosity.

"You know who gave us our Ammu?"

"No..." said Littpin.

"Your father," Abheera said.

Her eyes were filled with tears, and she longed to see Ammu again, but she was already home, and many thoughts passed through her mind.

"Ammu belonged to my father?"

"Maybe she knows me. She didn't try to attack me because I may not be a stranger to her."

"There is a connection between father and Ammu, which is why he wields an eagle pommel sword and wears the eagle claw chain." She rested in the home courtyard while the Captain and Abheera went for a bath in a nearby pond.

Chapter 41

TRUTH ALONE TRIUMPHS

As the Vaani Sena soldiers lowered the Tamnat flag at the city center entrance, a guard stationed in the watch tower spotted three approaching men, prompting him to sound an alarm. Although the trio was unarmed, one of them was shackled. Upon seeing the men, the watchtower guard exclaimed, "Our men are here! Open the gates!"

After the guard at the watchtower recognised the approaching men and ordered the gate to be opened, the weary trio entered the city, where the soldiers kindly offered them water and food. One of the guards inquired

"Why is he in chains.?"

"He had committed a crime while on duty."

Said one of the two soldiers who were previously held captive by the outlaws. The soldiers had not divulged the details of their ordeal to the guards as they were instructed by the woman who had rescued them to report the incident only in the presence of Lord Rakarna.

The guards arranged for a horse-drawn cart to transport the group to the Palace of Lord Rakarna. Once underway, they removed the chains and unwrapped the cloth from the rogue soldier's mouth. However, as some of the Vaani Sena soldiers near the palace were loyal to Chief Marutha, they had to be cautious not to appear as if they were presenting the rogue soldier to the court for confession.

Upon arriving at the palace, the soldiers requested entry to meet with Lord Rakarna but were informed by the palace guard that he was in a meeting and no one was allowed to enter. Undeterred, one of the soldiers appealed to the guard by stating,

"Soldier, it is a matter of Tamnat's security."

"The meeting is also of great importance to the security of the Bharatha country. A representative from the Crown is speaking with our Lord." Said the guard.

After leaving the entrance where the guards were stationed, the two soldiers retreated to a corner to devise a plan to meet Lord Rakarna. They decided that one of them would sneak into the palace courtroom via the back entrance, where there were fewer guards, while the other would keep the prisoner safe until the signal was given. The soldiers had initially suspected that the guard at the entrance was a loyalist of Chief Marutha, but they later discovered that he was not.

However, when one of the soldiers attempted to enter through the back entrance, he encountered three guards who were members of the elite King's Guard trained by the Bharatha Army. Knowing it was impossible to overpower them in close combat, the soldier opted to eavesdrop on the proceedings inside the courtroom by approaching an air hole meant for ventilation. From there, he could hear that some serious discussions were taking place.

"We can only provide one-third of our soldiers. Our province is also facing real threats from the outlaws." Said Lordof Tamnat.

A person bedecked in fancy chains and shining armour spoke,

"My Lord, the country is in grave danger, and we have received reports from spies that an attack is imminent. We must increase the number of Bharatha Army to ensure the safety of our nation. Please cooperate with us."

The soldier who had been eavesdropping concluded, "He must be the Crown's representative, so the guard at the entrance can be trusted."

He then returned to the entrance gate with his comrade and the rogue soldier. Before long, the Crown's representative and Tamnat's Chief of security emerged from the palace court. Taking advantage of the situation, one of the soldiers rushed into the courtroom.

The unexpected intrusion caught the guards off guard, and they followed the first soldier into the palace court. The second soldier also managed to sneak in, but he kept the rogue soldier hidden and safe from prying eyes. Suddenly, the King's Guard surrounded Lord Rakarna, forming a protective circle around him.

One of the soldiers shouted,

"My lord, Chief Marutha conspired with two soldiers to set the forest on fire!"

The guards apprehended the soldier and attempted to remove him from the courtroom, but Lord Rakarna intervened and ordered them to stop.

"Who are you, and from where are you coming?" Asked the lord

"My lord, we are the remaining soldiers of Commander Venkad's platoon." Said the soldier.

"Arrest them". Ordered chief Marutha.

And the guards came towards them, but Rakarna stopped them.

"Marutha, what are you doing?" Asked Rakarna.

"My lord, these are just allegations, and we shouldn't allow these allegations to go unpunished; they are also part of Venkad's conspiracy against the Lord."

"Why are you so defensive, Marutha? If you are innocent, we should hear what they have to say and decide later whether these are just allegations. We didn't even give Muthu a chance to speak when he was brought before us after the forest incident,"

Lord Rakarna stated, feeling guilty about how he had handled Muthu's case. He regretted not giving Muthu an opportunity to talk and console him when he had revealed that his brother had died. Lord Rakarna was aware that Marutha had manipulated him, and he wanted to make amends for his previous mistakes.

Lord Rakarna signalled the two soldiers to continue,

"My lord, it was Chief Marutha who conspired with three soldiers of our platoon,…" he explained the whole incident.

"But you don't have any evidence to prove this", said Chief Marutha.

"Yes, we have". said the other soldier.

Marutha was shocked. He thought,

"What will it be?"

"It was a foolproof plan".

"I had a plan, and three soldiers were part of it. But they were killed in a fight with the outlaws. If they hadn't died, my hitmen would have killed them anyway. It was a well-thought-out plan."

"Then show it, the proof." Ordered the Lord.

After one soldier signalled the other, the latter left the courtroom and retrieved the rogue soldier, leaving Chief Marutha stunned at the sight of the prisoner's survival. Desperate for a solution, Marutha attempted a last-ditch effort that ultimately proved to be the final blow to his own downfall.

He signalled his loyalist soldier to kill the rogue soldier, and the soldier rushed and slit the throat of the rogue soldier. The rogue soldier died in vain, and the courtroom was painted with the blood of the soldier.

After understanding the truth, Lord Rakarna ordered his elite King's guard to apprehend Marutha. However, Marutha's loyalists, who were present inside the courtroom, attempted to resist the King's guard but were ultimately defeated and killed. In the end, Marutha was arrested and taken to prison.

The King, in response to the rebellions happening throughout the country, deployed the elite King's guard to assist all the lords. Lord Rakarna, as part of his efforts to right the wrongs he had committed, ordered the release of Muthu from prison.

One group of soldiers went to free Muthu, while another took Marutha to prison. As fate would have it, Muthu and Marutha crossed paths, they came face to face, and Muthu uttered a single sentence:

"Truth alone triumphs."

Chapter 42
THE NIGHT JOKES

Abheera and the Captain returned home after their bath late at night. Littpin was sitting in the courtyard, gazing up at the sky, and they didn't want to disturb her since she seemed at peace for the first time in a long while.

Eventually, Dravas arrived in the courtyard, and Littpin noticed that he was concealing something behind his back.

"What is it, uncle?" Asked Littpin.

"Any guess?" Asked Dravas.

"Uncle, you always surprise me. Please reveal what surprise you have in store," said Littpin.

Dravas showed his magic, presented Littpin with a grey-coloured armour that featured an embossed eagle symbol on the back. The armour was incredibly lightweight, making it easier for Littpin to move flexibly. Littpin was amazed and expressed her gratitude towards Dravas for gifting her such a fantastic present.

"You are a good warrior like your father. Despite facing numerous losses and challenges, he never surrendered and always emerged as a heroic figure. You should follow his footsteps. Be resilient like him; never ever give up no matter what the odds are."

Littpin realised that Dravas was feeling nostalgic about his old friend, she lightened the mood by cracking a joke, saying

"Uncle, are you in the mood to give advice? Perhaps we should invite Abhi to join us."

Dravas started laughing and said,

"That was a good one, and you should keep this joke with you. It will befit your uncle Muthu also." His humorous comeback caused Littpin to burst into laughter.

Suddenly Littpin heard some movements outside the home, and she informed Dravas of it. But Dravas remained unaware of any noises outside, and he said,

"You have also started behaving like Abheera?"

"No uncle, but." She didn't complete her words.

"Nothing, dear. Trust me and have a good sleep. I have to sharpen the sword." Said Dravas.

Littpin went to bed, but she had many thoughts,

"What was that movement outside the home?"

"Is it some wild dogs?"

"Tomorrow, I have to spend some more time with Ammu."

"I will then get to know her connection with my father."

Littpin went to bed feeling very excited about the next day, and she gradually drifted off into a deep sleep. Meanwhile, Dravas spent the evening working on Venkad's sword to increase its sharpness, and by around midnight, he had finished the job, making the blade sharp enough to inflict severe cuts on Cobrython.

As Dravas was about to retire to bed, he suddenly heard Ammu's cries piercing through the midnight silence

"The poor girl might be hungry. I should get up early tomorrow and feed her," thought Dravas.

Chapter 43
THE SEARCH

Littpin woke up in the morning and freshened up before heading to the courtyard. There, she spotted Abheera and the Captain having a friendly sword fight.

As soon as they noticed her, they ceased their swordplay, and the Captain remarked,

"He is a skilled swordsman."

"Shall we recruit him, captain?" Asked Littpin with a laugh.

"He is already recruited, and he will lead the right flank of our army," said the Captain.

"Well, well, a Commander and a captain but with no army." Abheera mocked them back, and all of them burst into laughter.

"Littpin, shall we have a sword fight," asked Abheera.

"Since you have requested, of course, we can." Said Littpin.

Littpin went inside to take her sword and was amazed by its sharpness. When she returned to the courtyard with the sword in hand, the Captain and Abheera approached her to inspect the weapon. They, too, were astonished by the craftsmanship of Dravas.

"What instructions did father give you about this upgrade?" inquired Abheera.

"He isn't there in the room." Said Littpin.

"He is not there? It's impossible." Said Abheera.

"What? Why is it impossible? He might have gone outside." Said the Captain.

"Actually, Uncle," replied Abheera, "this is his usual time to wake up. He tends to work late into the night, so he doesn't typically rise early unless there is an urgent matter that requires his attention."

"Then let's not waste time; let's go look for him," said Littpin.

The Captain suggested that he would scour the city premises while asking Littpin and Abheera to search the Rockhill.

The Captain rushed towards the city, and Littpin and Abheera started to the Rockhill.

Abheera's heart felt heavy too, despite the arguments they had shared. He had great love for his father and felt immense pride whenever he saw Dravas in his military uniform. Dravas had served as a Captain in the Anantha Sena for many years before retiring. He had been Abheera's inspiration to join the Anantha Sena, and the thought of him being missing was a cause for concern.

"Abhi, don't worry. You have to be strong now." Littpin consoled him.

Observing Abheera's silence, Littpin understood that he needed some space to process his emotions. She was confident that Abheera would regain his composure soon enough.

The Captain began by visiting the settlement where his five soldiers resided and recruited them to aid in the search for Dravas.

As they combed the city premises, Littpin and Abheera traversed through the Rockhill valley. Suddenly, Littpin spotted something that sent chills down her spine. She glanced at Abheera, and he was stunned; he knelt down as tears rolled down his face.

They saw Dravas's body lying on the ground, his face down and his body soaked in blood.

Chapter 44

SHE IS FREE NOW

Littpin rushed towards Dravas, and she shouted,

"He is alive, Abhi."

Abheera got up and rushed towards Dravas, who was crying on the ground. Upon hearing Littpin's shouts, Dravas turned his head and gazed at Abheera and Littpin.

"What happened, father?" Abheera asked

"She is free now…" said Dravas.

Abheera understood that Dravas was speaking about Ammu; he said,

"She will come back, father. I will call her now." Abheera started calling her.

"Ammu…Ammu…Ammu…"

Littpin said,

"Abhi, hold on. See over there..." Littpin uttered with a shaky voice, and she gestured toward Ammu's cage.

The cage was shattered, and Ammu was lying on the ground, her gaze peaceful. Although her chain was intact, her body was crimson, drenched in blood. Abheera was in disbelief as he beheld the sight before him.

With tears rolling down his face, he cautiously approached Ammu. His steps were heavy, his motions were sluggish, and his breathing was steady.

"She is dead, right?" Asked Abheera.

Littpin couldn't answer it, she was crying, and tears flowed like a stream. Abheera touched Ammu's blood-bathed body and said,

"Ammu, you're finally free, but why didn't you take me with you?"

Abheera wailed, his voice echoing through Rockhill. Littpin came to him and held him tightly as he continued to cry.

At this point, the Captain and five soldiers arrived at Rockhill valley after their search in the city proved fruitless. The Captain said nothing and instructed the soldiers to bring a large red cloth and tools for digging the soil.

Approaching Dravas, who was seated on the ground with his eyes downcast, the Captain placed a hand on his shoulder. Dravas embraced the Captain and broke down in tears. Abheera watched this and felt remorseful for not consoling his father; perhaps his father needed someone to lean on, he thought.

"Captain, I should have listened to Abheera when he suspected the unusual movements here." Said Dravas.

"What are you saying, Dravas?" Asked the Captain.

"Yes, Captain. Cobrython's Snakes killed her." Said Dravas.

Abheera and Littpin were shocked hearing it. Abheera rushed to his father.

"Yes, Abhi, the voice you heard yesterday was the crawling of the snakes. The poor fought them bravely, but her chains..." said Dravas.

Abheera gazed at Ammu's claws and noticed patches of snake skin clinging to them. Furthermore, he observed bite marks on her legs and neck.

Littpin and the Captain exchanged glances and said,

"Captain, Cobrython has finally found us, and those snakes have confirmed the location also."

"Yes, Commander, we must get ready before he strikes with full might," said the Captain.

At that point in time, the soldiers came back carrying a sizable red cloth and equipment for digging the earth to create Ammu's ultimate resting spot. Subsequently, they began to dig the soil.

The Captain handed over the red cloth to Dravas, and Dravas wrapped the cloth around Ammu, and he sat near her. Abheera, Captain and Littpin also sat near Ammu.

The soldiers dug the grave, and they informed the Captain. The Captain said,

"Let's give her a warm send-off."

They lifted Ammu from the ground and slowly placed her in the grave. As a last rite of respect towards the dead, Captain asked everyone to put soil in her grave. Everyone bowed in respect, and the soldiers started covering the grave.

Suddenly Dravas asked the soldiers to stop and rushed towards her cage to take the food he had prepared for her. He placed that in her grave and said,

"She must be hungry."

They remained silent, shocked at the sudden death of Ammu.

Abheera remained looking at the grave of Ammu until it was filled with soil.

Chapter 45
THE CHIEF OF SECURITY

Muthu arrived at the palace court, where only Lord Rakarna was present. As soon as Lord Rakarna noticed him, he stood up and walked towards Muthu. Their eyes met briefly, and then Lord Rakarna clapped his hands, prompting a king's guard to enter the room with a plate covered by a red cloth. The guard approached Lord Rakarna and uncovered the plate, revealing Muthu's daggers, which had been confiscated by the palace guards when Muthu reported an incident in the deep forest.

Lord Rakarna took the daggers and handed them back to Muthu, expressing his apologies.

"Muthu, please forgive me for my ignorance. As a ruler, I shouldn't have acted in haste. I regret my hasty decisions."

"My Lord, you don't need to be guilty. You have rectified your mistake, and that is what the people expect from a ruler, to acknowledge errors and take corrective measures." Said Muthu.

They mourned the death of Venkad and talked about dispatching troops to the North of the Country. They also deliberated on the immediate threat posed by Cobrython and his army of snakes.

"My Lord, Cobrython and his army of snakes are mighty, and we should deploy the Vaani Sena to thwart their attack plan on us.", Muthu said.

"But Muthu, our numbers are already reduced, and our chief of security is deployed in the North."

Said the Lord, and suddenly he had a thought and decided to appoint Muthu as the new Chief of Security. Initially, Muthu was not in agreement, but eventually, he acceded to the Lord's request.

The Lord then inquired about a woman who had visited Muthu in prison a few days ago, as reported by his guards.

"An old friend, my Lord," Muthu replied.

Without further questioning, the Lord bestowed the title of Chief of Security upon Muthu, who officially assumed the position.

After assuming his new role in the court of Tamnat, Muthu departed and made his way to the Chief of Security's chamber. There, he retrieved a small piece of cloth typically used for messaging and proceeded to write a message before affixing his seal upon it. Muthu then commanded the raven keeper to dispatch the message to the Lord of Malnat.

Chapter 46
LORD MANIKTA

"We have to meet lord Manikta," said the Captain.

"But how can we leave Abheera and Dravas uncle like this?" Asked Littpin.

Littpin was also grieving over Ammu's passing. The previous night, she had contemplated the possibility of meeting Ammu again and spending some quality time together. However, fate had other plans, and Littpin's happiness was short-lived.

"Commander, we have to hold back our emotions; there is a war coming, and the enemy is much stronger than us," Captain said.

Abheera overheard their conversation and commented,

"Littpin, he is correct. Cobrython has traced our location and is likely to launch an attack soon on us."

And he continued,

"I will lead the right flank, as the Captain said earlier. Correct, uncle?"

"Yes, Abheera", Captain approved.

The Captain was aware that having Abheera with them added another motive for revenge to the impending battle.

Subsequently, Littpin and the Captain set out to meet the Lord of Malnat, instructing their five soldiers to remain on guard at Abheera's residence.

Upon arriving at Lord Manikta's palace, Littpin and the Captain requested permission to meet with him. The guards requested their names and address, to which they replied that they were from Tamnat. The guards then asked for their travel certificates, which were required to track the movement of people entering and exiting the provinces. However, Littpin and the Captain did not possess their travel certificates. Even if they had them, their entry into Malnat would not have been recorded as they had entered the land illegally.

"We don't have the certificate with us, soldier," said the Captain.

Since they didn't have their travel certificates, the guards grew suspicious and arrested Littpin and the Captain. However, the Chief of Security of Malnat, Ashwadarsh, arrived at that moment to meet with the Lord and inquired about the situation with the guards.

"Chief, they want to meet the lord, but they don't have their travel certificates with them", reported the guard.

The Chief of Security ordered the guards to detain and imprison Littpin and the Captain.

"Chief, I am Sajeera, a Captain of the Vaani Sena, and I have an urgent matter to discuss with the Lord," pleaded the Captain.

The Chief replied

"Then show me your travel certificate; it must have all your details", he continued. "I don't have time to waste here, and I have to meet the lord urgently,". Saying this, the Chief rushed back to the palace.

As they were being taken away to the prison, Littpin noticed that the Chief of Security was holding a scroll of cloth with the seal of the Chief of Security of Tamnat. Meanwhile, the soldiers escorted Littpin and the Captain to their cell, and the Chief approached Lord Manikta.

He bowed and said,

"My lord, we have a message from Tamnat." Chief handed over the sealed message to the King's guard, and they gave it to the Lord; he opened the seal and started reading it.

Littpin and the Captain were detained in separate cells facing each other. Littpin spoke up and said,

"Captain, did you see the message that the Chief of Security of Malnat was holding? It had the seal of the Chief of Security of Tamnat."

The Captain replied, "Yes, I saw it, but I don't know what the message could be about."

Littpin speculated, "Perhaps it has something to do with us. Chief Marutha might have convinced Chief Ajral to put a lookout notice for us."

"But Marutha doesn't know if we are alive or not," Captain replied.

"But he does have spies working for him. What if they found us?" Asked Littpin.

"That is a possibility, Commander," Captain said.

The sound of approaching soldiers' footsteps caught Littpin and the Captain's attention. The soldiers arrived and unlocked their cells, escorting them to the palace court. And they suspected that they were about to be get transported back to Tamnat.

They were produced in the court, and they bowed before the Lord.

"Littpin and Captain Sajeera", lord Manikta told their names. They were astonished and saddened by the turn of events because they thought they were about to get transported back to Tamnat.

"Don't be scared; you are not going to be arrested. Anantha Sena will fight alongside you." Said lord Manikta.

Littpin and Captain were in shock, and they looked at each other in disbelief. The Chief of security of Malnat looked at them and nodded with a smile. They couldn't believe the unexpected turn of the fate.

"Your offer brings us great joy, my Lord. However, I must ask if you are aware of our adversary," Littpin inquired.

"Yes, Littpin. The scroll in the possession of the Chief of Security has detailed accounts of all the events and the involvement of Cobrython," replied Lord Manikta.

"But Ajral doesn't know anything about Cobrython." Said the Captain with disbelief.

"Captain, Chief Ajral is on deputation to the North of the country. The Chief of security of Tamnat is your Uncle, Muthu," Lord Manikta informed Littpin.

The Captain and Littpin were overwhelmed with joy as they also believed in the principle of

"Truth alone triumphs."

Chapter 47
THE SHEEP EATER

"But the problem is, our current force of soldiers is limited to only one-third, as the remaining troops have been sent to the North." Said Ashwadarsh.

Upon hearing this, Littpin responded, "Chief, with all due respect, the current army strength will not be sufficient. The enemy is powerful, and we will require more soldiers to defeat them."

"We know that Littpin and the Vaani Sena will join us soon, so that we will be in good numbers." Said lord Manikta.

"Lord, it will take a day for the entire Vaani Sena to arrive here,"

said the Captain, aware that a large army would take more time to travel than a small group due to the need to carry a large number of weapons and equipment, as well as the inclusion of horse carts, which would also slow down the movement of troops.

"We hope Cobrython will not attack before that." Said the Lord.

Littpin alerted the Lord,

"My Lord, I believe they are already here, and an attack may happen anytime. We had an incident last night at Rockhill where a horse belonging to us was killed by snakes."

However, she refrained from mentioning anything about Ammu, as her presence here was a secret known only to Dravas and Abheera. If the Lord found out about Ammu, there could be an investigation, which could potentially lead to the exhumation of her body for analysis. Littpin did not want that to happen.

"Let's hope that they don't attack today. Anyway, I will deploy thirty platoons to the Rockhill along with you." Lord Manikta told.

Both Littpin and Captain agreed to this plan, and as they were preparing to leave the palace court, a man in a shabby dress entered and bowed before Lord Manikta.

Littpin wondered how the shabbily dressed man managed to enter the palace court since guards only permitted soldiers and nobles. However, the Captain recognised the man,

"It is a spy, Commander," Captain informed Littpin.

The spy was hesitant to speak, as there were strangers inside the palace court.

"They are our people," said the Lord

The spy addressed the Lord, saying,

"My Lord, a Shepherd boy and his family was found dead on the forest border, and their sheep are also missing. Additionally, many sheep have disappeared, and people are afraid of the Sheep Eater."

"Akshuru," said Littpin and Captain together.

"What was the cause of their death?" Asked the Chief of security.

"Snake bites, my lord." Said the spy.

"So, they are here." Said the Lord. He asked the spy to leave.

"Ashwadarsh, call all the captains, brief them about the situation, and ask the border guards to keep the borders closed." Lord alerted the Chief.

After Ashwadarsh bowed to Lord Manikta and left to brief the platoon captains, the Lord turned his attention to Littpin and the Captain, who appeared saddened by the news of Akshuru's death. They acknowledged the importance of Akshuru's help, as they wouldn't have made it to Malnat without him.

"We must reach Rockhill soon. Our friends are alone there, my LordLLittpin said with urgency.

"Littpin, you can leave by evening; only then our troops will be ready troops for the battle." Said the Lord.

"No, my Lord, it's too late. I cannot wait; I have to be with them." Said Littpin.

"I will send five of my own personal guards with you. The road can be perilous, and with just the two of you, it may not be safe," Lord Manikta offered.

The Captain raised a concern, "My Lord, the King's guards are primarily deployed for your protection. Would it be wise to divert them for this task?"

"Captain, do you forget what my role was before becoming the lord?" said Lord Manikta with a wink on his face.

Chapter 48
THE BEGGARS

Littpin, the Captain, and the King's guard embarked on their journey towards Dravas's home, riding at a swift pace. The memories of Akshuru weighed heavily on both Littpin's and the Captain's minds.

"He was a good lad. He was never a part of this war."

"Whenever there is war, the innocent people also suffer, which is very unfair."

"They say everything is fair in love and war. But I cannot agree with that."

Littpin was drowned in her thoughts, and suddenly she heard someone calling,

"Help us; please help us."

"Help us, please."

She ordered the party to halt, and the Captain said,

"Beggars, Commander... let's go."

"What if they are beggars, Captain? They are only asking for help." Littpin said.

She looked at the beggars; there were three of them, and one among them was a lady. Littpin approached them and asked what they wanted.

"Madam, it has been two days since we've had a meal. Could you please provide us with some food?" the woman requested.

"Oh, I am very sorry, we are not carrying food with us. I will give you the money to buy enough food. Is that okay?" Asked Littpin.

"Thank you, my lady. The Lord will always be there for you," said she.

Littpin was taken aback by the woman's words. She wondered why the woman had said, "Lord will always be there for you," instead of "God will always be there for you."

Then she realised that the woman and her family lived in poverty and might not know the difference between the two. The woman attempted to hug Littpin, but the King's guard intervened. Littpin, being a kind-hearted person, asked the guard not to stop the woman. The woman hugged Littpin and left.

Littpin watched them leave,

"Does they look like they haven't eaten for two days?"

"I don't think so."

"Maybe they have tricked me into getting some cash. But that's okay. They could do much more with that money than I could do with it."

She started riding faster as she rode towards Dravas's home.

Chapter 49

BATTLE READY

When Littpin and the Captain arrived at Dravas's home, they were taken aback by the sight of Dravas, Abheera, and five soldiers dressed for battle, along with several boxes neatly arranged in the courtyard.

Littpin asked,

"Why are you in battle uniform, Abhi.?"

"They are here, Littpin. They are up there in the Rockhill." Replied Abheera.

"How do you know that?" Littpin asked.

"We have heard the loud hiss of Cobrython." Said Dravas.

"We have to go there immediately," said Abheera.

"But Abhi, the troops are yet to come. Lord Manikta has ordered the deployment of thirty platoons here. Let them come. Then we will March ahead." Said Littpin.

"No, dear, we don't have the privilege of time here. The enemy is already here, and if we don't stop them, they will enter the city and kill many innocent civilians." Said Dravas.

The Captain concurred with Dravas's argument, leaving Littpin to launch the attack alone, without any support. After a short while, Littpin emerged from inside, wearing the new armour crafted by Dravas.

"Commander, please deliver the war speech," the Captain instructed Littpin.

She ordered the soldiers to assemble in formation, and they eagerly awaited their commander's address before the battle.

"Valiant warriors of Bharatha, though we may be outnumbered, we are in no way inferior to our foes. Soldiers, our enemy may be formidable, but so are we. We have fought to safeguard our homeland and our people, and we will continue to do so. We have shed blood to uphold justice, and we are prepared to do so again, but we shall never surrender, for we are the fearless defenders of our nation."

"Soldiers, raise your swords...."

"Sarparna Sthabdh"

"Sarparna Sthabdh"

"Sarparna Sthabdh", the soldiers shouted the war cry in unison.

The King's guards were perplexed by the unfamiliar war cry, but they nonetheless rallied behind it, recognising the power of the emotion to unite soldiers and raise morale. The Captain beamed with pride at Littpin following her impassioned address.

Littpin then approached Abheera and inquired,

"What was in those boxes.?"

"Weapons", Said Abheera

Abheera opened all the boxes, and Littpin was astonished by the weapons, which were entirely new to her.

Dravas approached Littpin and said,

"Littpin, these weapons will help us win against the odds. We may not have numbers, but these are enough to defend our positions or even to go for an offensive attack."

Dravas took a bow and arrow from a box,

"This bow is very accurate, and it has a long range. The arrow is sharp and made up of the same alloy as your sword." Said Dravas.

Taking up her bow and arrow, Littpin directed her aim towards a nearby tree, testing its potency and precision.

Upon releasing the arrow, it penetrated through the tree and struck the adjacent one, leaving her awestruck by its astounding accuracy and formidable strength.

"Great uncle. This is great." Said Littpin.

Littpin instructed the King's guards to adopt the bow and arrow as their primary armament, recognising that as protectors of the King, they could not be assigned to frontline combat.

Dravas then unveiled a larger version of the bow, too unwieldy to be carried by hand, which could launch six arrows in quick succession without needing to be reloaded. Littpin deemed this weapon to be invaluable in vanquishing the snake army of Cobrython and directed the King's guards to master its use.

Dravas then revealed the contents of another box, which contained numerous round-shaped objects. He said,

"This is called pokala; this will emit smoke upon breaking, causing the enemy's sight to be blurred, enabling us to seize the opportunity to make our escape.."

Littpin asked each soldier to carry one or two pokala.

Then there was another small box, which Dravas did not open, and Littpin asked,

"What is in that box, uncle?"

"These implements are necessary to rectify any malfunctions that may arise in the bow machine." He then secured the small container onto his belt.

"Soldiers, let's rock the Rockhill."

Shouted Littpin, and they marched towards the Rockhill with their war cry,

"Sarparna Sthabdh"

"Sarparna Sthabdh"

Chapter 50
VENGEANCE VS JUSTICE

Arriving at the valley's edge, Littpin instructed her troops to proceed in stealth mode. The sun was setting, painting the entirety of Rockhill in a warm orange hue. Despite scanning the area thoroughly, they detected no sign of enemy activity, and an eerie stillness pervaded the surroundings.

"They must be present here; otherwise, Rockhill would never be this silent," Dravas whispered.

"Yes, father."

Abheera agreed with his father.

Littpin ordered her soldiers to take cover behind the trees and prepare their weapons. Understanding that they were vastly outnumbered, she formulated a new strategy: to defend the Valley side, the pathway that linked the city to the top of Rockhill. By holding this position, they could prevent Cobrython's forces from entering the city and buy time for the thirty platoons of Anantha Sena to arrive. Once the reinforcements reached them, they could engage Cobrython's army in the open fields of

Rockhill, where their superior numbers would be an advantage.

The Captain said,

"Commander, I see no enemy movements here. We need to go to the top of the Rockhill and check for their presence."

"No, Captain. We cannot win an open battle with their army." Littpin said.

"And there is no use if we wait here also. We have to go there and fight him," said Abheera.

Captain sensed the rage inside Abheera, and he knew that revenge and vengeance would only invite catastrophic failure.

The Captain said,

"Revenge and Vengeance revenge could weaken a warrior's resolve and cloud their judgment, preventing them from standing up for justice."

After completing these words, he looked at both Abheera and Littpin.

Littpin realised that the Captain's words also applied to her desire for vengeance against Cobrython for her father's death. She asked herself,

"Why am I fighting this war?"

"What am I fighting for?"

"Is it vengeance?"

"What if my father was not killed by Cobrython? Then would I have fought this war?"

"So, am I fighting this war for a personal reason?"

These thoughts drowned her, and she lost her confidence.

Dravas noticed a shift in Littpin's demeanour and approached her, inquiring,

"Littpin, what's going on with you?

"Uncle, am I not a good leader? Am I fighting this war out of personal vendetta? Is it vengeance?" Asked Littpin.

"Littpin, consider this: Would you not fight against Cobrython if he were to kill a poor shepherd boy? And would you not fight against Cobrython if he and his army were to slaughter the sheep of the shepherds, which is their only means of livelihood?"

"Yes, Uncle, I will fight him," Littpin said.

"Then you are a true leader, a true citizen, and a good daughter". Dravas replied.

Littpin relaxed after hearing Dravas's reply.

"I am not fighting for vengeance."

"I will fight for justice."

Said Littpin to herself.

Chapter 51
THE FIRST WAVE

Abheera was losing his patience, he said,

"I am going to the top of the Rockhill. There is no use in waiting here. I will go there and see if any movement is up there."

"No, Abhi, we don't know what's up there." Said Littpin.

"That is why I said I will go and check." Said Abheera.

The Captain interrupted and said,

"I will also go along with him, commander."

Littpin wouldn't allow Abheera to go alone due to concerns for his safety, but since the Captain, a seasoned warrior, was accompanying him, she agreed.

Abheera and the Captain started towards the top of the Rockhill. They have reached the top of the Rockhill, and it's already dark.

Upon reaching the top, which was already dark, the Captain directed Abheera to a group of rocks where a pile of something was seen. Upon closer inspection, they discovered a shocking sight of bones from a large animal.

Although the Captain realized they were the remains of Ammu, he chose not to inform Abheera about it. It appeared that the outlaws had dug up Ammu's body to provide food for Cobrython's army.

"They must be here", whispered the Captain.

"Uncle, it is difficult to find them here, Rockhill top is vast in area, and there are many crevices and small caves here and there. Where will you find them?" Asked Abheera.

"We don't have to find them; they will find us." Said, Captain.

Suddenly they heard it.

The drum beats of the Anantha Sena marching towards the Rockhill.

Unexpected movements caught their attention as about ten outlaws emerged from an artificially dug pit on the Rockhill. Abheera and the Captain took cover behind a large tree, observing as the outlaws made their way towards the valley side accompanied by five enormous snakes, leaving Abheera stunned by their size. Even more surprising was the appearance of a second group of thirty outlaws and fifteen snakes following closely behind the first. This was the first time Abheera had ever seen these giant creatures.

After seeing the terrified Abheera, Captain asked,

"If you are scared after seeing his army, what would you do when you see king Cobrython."

Abheera remained silent for some time, and when he regained his normalcy, he asked,

"Shouldn't we go and help them, Captain.?"

"No, Abheera, we cannot follow them. Don't worry, all forty outlaws and twenty snakes are heading straight into a trap. If we follow them, our soldiers won't be able to shoot arrows at the enemy, as we would be in their range. Therefore, we should stay here and see if there's a second wave." Said the Captain.

Littpin instructed her soldiers to hold their fire until the first wave of outlaws and snakes had passed their position. The King's guard readied their arrows, preparing for the right moment to release them upon the enemy. Meanwhile, Dravas prepared the large weapon and waited for Littpin's command to fire.

Chapter 52
DON'T LOOK UP

The Captain and Abheera were scanning the area for any signs of movement, but after the first wave, there was complete silence. Suddenly, the Captain felt something odd about the tree they were using as cover. He pressed his ear against the trunk and heard a faint but distinct heartbeat. As he looked up, all he could see was a strange red and green glow in the darkness.

"Run, Abheera, run."

The Captain shouted, pulled Abheera along with him and started running.

Abheera was about to look up, and the Captain said,

"Don't look up. Just run…"

The Captain was aware that if Abheera caught a glimpse of King Cobrython, he might be paralyzed with fear and unable to run. Even the bravest warriors couldn't see King Cobrython without feeling terror, and Abheera was no exception. They could hear a loud hissing noise behind them, but Abheera had no idea what was happening. He began to curse the moment he had decided to investigate the Rockhill.

"Stupid, stupid,..." he called himself while running towards the valley side.

The forty outlaws and the twenty Cobras of the first wave have now crossed Littpin. She signalled the soldiers to fire at the snakes first, and the soldiers fired, and it was utterly silent operation.

Littpin was amazed at the accuracy of her soldiers' bow skills as they managed to take down all twenty cobras with just three rounds of firing.

"What a weapon!" She told herself.

The forty outlaws didn't even get the slightest clue of what happened. Before the forty outlaws could react, a hail of arrows struck them, killing them instantly. The precision of the attack made military action appear seamless.

She was relieved that the first wave was dealt with, and she signalled the soldiers to hold their position and stay alert for any potential second wave.

The sound of drums grew louder, and in the distance, they could see troops approaching with torches. Suddenly, Littpin heard Abheera shouting for help, and she attempted to leave her position, but Dravas prevented her from doing so.

"No, Littpin, you will compromise the complete mission, don't leave your post now. This post is advantageous for us, and we could kill their whole army by attacking from here." Said Dravas.

Dravas, too, had heard Abheera's desperate cry for help, but he understood the gravity of their mission and the potential consequences if they were to abandon their posts. He knew that the safety of their entire country was at stake and that personal losses had to be set aside for the greater good.

However, Abheera's cries suddenly stopped, sending chills down the spines of Littpin and Dravas. The silence that followed was ominous and terrifying. Dravas glanced at Littpin and saw that she was paralyzed with fear, unable to move or speak.

Visuals of her father being swallowed by Cobrython passed through her mind. she clenched her fists and shouted,

"Cobrython…"

She ordered the soldiers to leave their posts and advance to the top of the Rockhill.

Chapter 53
THE BATTLE OF ROCKHILL

Upon reaching the top of the Rockhill, Littpin, Dravas, and the soldiers caught sight of King Cobrython, who was standing in the open field. His eyes shone with a red and green glow.

Littpin said to Dravas,

"Light up, uncle."

Dravas dipped an arrow into oil, ignited its tip, and aimed it at the tree that Abheera and the Captain had used as cover. As soon as the arrow hit the tree, flames quickly spread, illuminating the top of the Rockhill. From this vantage point, they could now see the massive army of King Cobrython in full force. The army comprised over five hundred outlaws and three hundred large cobras, along with various weapons and materials, including catapults.

"Finally, the Battle of Rockhill begins..." said Littpin.

Littpin asked the soldiers to nock the arrows. The five soldiers of the King's guard tightened their arrows, and they waited for her order.

Littpin's fists remain clenched, her teeth grinding with anger and a burning desire for revenge. She had tried to control her thirst for vengeance earlier, thanks to the Captain's calming words. However, the Captain's death at the hands of Cobrython, and now Abheera's death, had only made her more furious. She is determined to avenge her father, the Captain, Abheera, and Akshuru, the innocent shepherd boy.

Meanwhile, Dravas is also prepared, holding a massive bow machine and aiming at Cobrython. King Cobrython recognizes the threat posed by the machine and decides not to advance his army. Instead, he plans to crush the machine to remove the biggest obstacle to his victory.

"Cobrython is not ordering the attack, and he is retreating, Commander." Said one of the King's guards.

"No, he is not." Said Dravas.

Littpin realized that Cobrython was not ordering an attack because if they advanced, they would come under the range of archers.

She said,

"You are already under our range."

Upon Littpin's signal, the archers unleashed a volley of arrows, causing Cobrython to be taken aback as fifteen of his outlaws were swiftly killed by the attack. This made Cobrython aware of the high penetrating power of the arrows, and he realized that if his army were to be standing in formation, just one arrow could take down up to three men, which was evident by the recent attack that killed fifteen men with only five arrows.

Cobrython was aware that he needed to preserve the number of outlaws since they were already diminished compared to the troops marching towards Rockhill. He gauged the number of Anantha Sena by feeling the vibrations of the ground made by their movement.

Cobrython commanded the outlaws and snakes to break away from their formations. Suddenly, something swift grazed past his eye, leaving a shallow cut, and he realized that Dravas had shot an arrow from the large bow machine. He hissed loudly at Dravas, but Dravas remained composed and fired another arrow, which Cobrython managed to evade.

It wasn't easy to aim at Cobrython because his two heads were constantly moving, even when he stood still.

Littpin was astonished to witness Cobrython's fully grown teeth as it screamed with its two wide-open mouths.

"What a filthy creature?" She said to herself.

Suddenly there were some movements in the bushes. Without warning, two cobra snakes attacked Dravas from the right flank, aiming to destroy the bow machine. The five soldiers of the Vaani Sena quickly sprang into action and fought off the snakes with their impressive combat skills, which they had learned from Venkad and Muthu during the first battle with Cobrython. Even Dravas was amazed by their abilities. Although they were able to save Dravas, the bow machine was destroyed by the snakes. The soldiers realized that this was a suicide mission ordered by Cobrython.

Littpin understood they were now in a weak spot with the big bow machine gone. She asked Dravas,

"Uncle, can we repair the machine?"

"It will take time." Said Dravas

"I will get you the time, uncle." Said Littpin.

"We don't have much time. He will order the attack now, and I can't stay here idle by repairing the machine and you all fighting with them. I already lost my friend, my son, and I can't bear any more loss." Said Dravas.

Littpin could understand his feeling. Despite Abheera and Dravas's frequent disagreements, they cared for each other, and Abheera's death would have been a significant loss for Dravas.

Subsequently, Cobrython ordered his army to advance, and a hundred outlaws and fifty snakes began moving forward.

Littpin commanded the archers to shoot at will and instructed the five Vaani Sena soldiers to prepare to charge.

The archers were able to take down all fifty Cobras due to their agility and speed. However, they refrained from targeting the outlaws as they knew they could easily defeat them in close combat, unlike the snakes, which posed a more significant threat.

As the outlaws approached, Littpin ordered the archers to switch to swords. She led the charge, jumping towards the incoming outlaws and killing two of them mid-air with her eagle pommel sword. Her swift movements and skillful sword strikes led to a surge in the number of kills.

Upon witnessing the attack by Littpin, Cobrython ordered ten Cobras to charge at the King's guard. Two of the guards fell, unable to resist the swift attack. In response, Littpin arrived and quickly sliced off the heads of the two Cobras.

Her body was already covered in the blood of her enemies, and her thirst for vengeance fueled her desire to kill. She attacked the Cobras like a fierce warrior and managed to defeat all ten of them. However, driven by rage and seeking revenge, she charged towards

Cobrython, losing sight of what was happening on the battlefield.

Cobrython had given the signal for another attack, but Littpin was unaware of it as she was consumed by her vengeance. Over fifty snakes attacked the soldiers, resulting in the King's guard and two soldiers from Vaani Sena falling.

As she neared Cobrython, she leaped to strike his head, but he evaded it and delivered a powerful blow with his tail, knocking Littpin to the ground and causing her sword to slip from her hand. Without a weapon, Littpin was defenceless when two outlaws swung their swords at her, but the attack was blocked by the eagle pommel sword wielded by the Captain.

"Rise, Commander." The Captain said, and he killed both the outlaws in a single strike.

Littpin was happy to see the Captain alive. She inquired,

"Abhi?"

But the Captain's eyes were downcast, and he said,

"I couldn't save him, Commander. As Cobrython came to attack us, we ran towards the valley side, but we got separated in the middle, and unfortunately, Cobrython didn't follow me. He followed poor Abhi," he said, choking back sobs.

Littpin didn't utter a word.

Chapter 54

THE SCROLL

Dravas arrived with the three remaining soldiers of the Vaani Sena. Upon seeing the Captain, Dravas looked at him expectantly. The Captain was able to discern what Dravas was inquiring about, and without the need for words, he simply lowered his gaze. Dravas understood the message and remained silent.

"Commander, we have to retreat," said one soldier.

Only then Littpin realized that they had suffered a tremendous loss.

The Captain took something from the ground and checked it.

"What is it, Captain?"

Littpin asked the Captain in a subdued tone, reflecting her emotional and physical losses in both the battle and personal life.

"It is a scroll, Commander." Said, Captain.

"How did it come here?" Littpin asked.

"It had fallen from you when you fell on the ground." Said, Captain.

"From me? No way. I am seeing it for the first time." Said Littpin.

Littpin took the scroll from the Captain, and she opened it, and something was drawn on it. Before she could interpret what it was, Cobrython and his army advanced.

"Retreat, Retreat." Ordered Littpin.

Pushed to the end of the cliff with Cobrython and his army advancing rapidly, the group found themselves with only two options: jump from the cliff and face certain death, or fight the enemy and accept their own demise. They had all come to terms with the possibility of death and were prepared for one final battle.

Cobrython halted midway and ordered the outlaws to kill the soldiers and catch Littpin alive. Cobrython's thirst for revenge remained unquenched, and he relentlessly hissed at Littpin, who was now in danger of being captured alive or killed by the Cobrython himself.

Meanwhile, a group of approximately twenty outlaws charged towards Littpin and her small group, unaware that even a single soldier from the Vaani Sena could take down up to ten of them before succumbing. Now, with three Vaani Sena soldiers, along with the Captain, Dravas, and the formidable Littpin, the odds were not in the outlaws' favour. The Captain said,

"They will never learn, right?"

They laughed, raised their swords, and welcomed the incoming attack.

Littpin was also worried that this attack might be a decoy and that Cobrython may have another plan in mind. Even in the midst of the battle with the outlaws, she kept her gaze fixed on Cobrython.

As Littpin focused on Cobrython, her attention to the fight waned, allowing an outlaw to land a cut on her right hand. Infuriated, she thrust her eagle pommel sword through his heart, killing him instantly. With all twenty outlaws defeated, they prepared for the next wave of attack from Cobrython. Seeing his remaining forces, Cobrython signalled for them to attack. The Captain remarked,

"Now their brain is lit up."

"Soldiers, we fought together, and we will die together. It is glorious to die while doing one's duty." Littpin said.

"Aye, Commander," said them.

"Soldiers, Sarparna Sthabdh". Shouted Littpin.

"Sarparna Sthabdh, Sarparna Sthabdh".

"Sarparna Sthabdh, Sarparna Sthabdh"

The atmosphere echoed with Sarparna Sthabdh, and the sky was filled with many stars. The outlaws looked at the sky and started retreating towards their earlier location.

The twinkling lights that they had seen were not stars but rather the flaming arrows launched by thirty platoons of Anantha Sena, led by Ashwadarsh. Similarly, the sound that they had earlier heard was not an echo but the battle cry of Anantha Sena. The fire arrows illuminated the entire area until they hit the ground, killing many retreating outlaws. The remaining outlaws gathered around Cobrython, who let out a loud hiss that reverberated throughout Rockhill. Littpin and her team felt a sense of relief upon seeing the Anantha Sena taking over the Rockhill. However, they knew that the war was far from over.

Littpin and the Captain were approached by Chief Ashwadarsh, who asked,

"Afraid, were you?"

The Captain chuckled and replied, "Ha ha."

He then asked, "Chief, how did you arrive at the perfect time?"

"We were getting slower, so we abandoned the drums to increase the speed of troop movement," explained the Chief.

"I see. That's why the drumming suddenly stopped," said the Captain.

"And you must have been anxious at that moment, am I right?" asked the Chief.

The Captain replied to the Chief,

"We would have liked to be tensed, but Cobrython kept us occupied all the time, so we didn't have the chance."

Everyone laughed upon hearing the Captain's response. Despite intentionally keeping the soldiers engaged to boost their morale, he felt a sense of guilt within himself. The Captain believed that he was responsible for Abheera's death.

Despite receiving prior briefing, the soldiers of the Anantha Sena were taken aback by the sight of Cobrython and his snake army. Chief Ashwadarsh noticed this and believed that the soldiers required a motivational speech before the upcoming battle.

Cobrython gestured for the outlaws to retreat towards the rear of their formation, as their numbers had been considerably reduced. He was now contemplating a new strategy since he couldn't directly engage the nine hundred skilled soldiers of the Anantha Sena.

The Chief analyzed the moves of Cobrython closely, but he didn't understand why Cobrython ordered the outlaws to stand at the rear side of the formation. Chief then looked at Littpin, who was busy with the scroll in her hand.

A sparkling light was in her eyes after she read the message on the scroll. Littpin smiled and said,

"The Lord will always be with me."

Chapter 55

THE LAST WAVE

Chief Ashwadarsh commenced his battle speech, "Soldiers, Today we may win or lose.

Today might be the last day for us.

But one thing is sure, that today we will create history.

Soldiers, raise your swords, heads high,

Sarparna Sthabdh."

He concluded his speech with the rallying cry of "Sarparna Sthabdh."

And soldiers chanted the war cry,

"Sarparna Sthabdh Sarparna Sthabdh"

"Sarparna Sthabdh Sarparna Sthabdh"

Dravas, who was leading the right flank, was in mourning after the sudden death of Abheera

"Uncle, you please go with the central formation." Said Littpin.

"No, dear, he was excited to lead the right flank. When he said to me about that, there was a spark inside his eye. Most of the time, I will scold him, and rarely, I appreciate him. He loved me very much. He also wanted to become a soldier, but when he got the chance, my son is no more in this world."

Dravas saved his tears to gain strength from them. The Captain joined them; he said,

"We will avenge Abheera's death".

With their swords pointed towards the ground, they vowed to avenge Abheera's death. Both Littpin and Dravas joined in on this vow. It was the Captain who had previously advised Littpin and Abheera to prioritize fighting for justice over seeking vengeance. However, even he had now come forward to avenge Abheera's untimely death. Despite the short time that had passed since Abheera's passing, he had already earned a special place in their hearts.

Cobrython refrained from commanding an attack towards their army, prompting the Chief to order the advance team to initiate an attack against Cobrython's formation. The advance team, consisting of five platoons, adopted the trident formation and charged forward towards Cobrython and his army.

During the charge, the tree that had been set alight by Dravas fell, causing the fire to extinguish and plunging Rockhill back into darkness. While the standing army had torches to provide light, the advance team did not carry any as it would hamper their mobility. Moreover, the tree that was on fire had previously provided sufficient light for the area.

A moment of silence enveloped the troops until the unexpected occurred - the entire Rockhill was once again illuminated, but not due to a burning tree. The sudden turn of events sent a shiver down the spine of Anantha Sena's standing troops.

Littpin and the Captain exchanged a horrified glance as they witnessed the entire advance team being set ablaze by the enemy. The screams of the soldiers reverberated throughout Rockhill, and the stench of burnt flesh filled the air. However, their screams were short-lived as they quickly resorted to slitting their throats as a means of escaping the excruciating pain. Despite the soldiers' rigorous training, this was protocol in the case of an imminent capture or extreme suffering.

Without even engaging in combat with the enemy, one hundred and fifty soldiers lost their lives. In an attempt to retaliate, Littpin requested Dravas to light up another tree at Rockhill. Upon scrutinizing the enemy's actions, Littpin realized that the Cobras had stored oil in their mouths. As soon as the soldiers came within their range, the Cobras sprayed the oil all over the soldiers, and the outlaws set the entire advance team on fire.

Looking at the Chief, Littpin was taken aback to see him stupefied by the tragic loss of his soldiers. The entire advance team was burned alive, and the Chief couldn't bear the sight of the one hundred and fifty soldiers burning, screaming, and ultimately resorting to taking their own lives.

The Captain came to Littpin and said,

"Commander, you have to take charge of Anantha Sena. The Chief needs help."

Realizing the need to take charge of Anantha Sena, Littpin gave orders for the remaining twenty-five platoons to form the Suchakra formation.

Suchakra formation is an offensive formation where the soldiers form a rotating circle with three concentric circles of varying sizes. The outermost circle comprises soldiers wielding shields and spears to create a defensive line while also being able to attack. The middle circle comprises soldiers equipped with swords for close combat, while the innermost circle comprises archers and commanders.

As Littpin stood within the inner circle of the Suchakra formation, she observed that the soldiers in the outer circle were unable to break through Cobrython's formation due to their ordinary iron weapons. She alerted Captain and Dravas to this fact, and together they developed a plan of action.

When the Suchakra formation eventually approached Cobrython's army, the enemy was taken aback by an unexpected manoeuvre from inside the formation. Littpin, Dravas, Captain, and three soldiers from Vaani Sena leaped out of the formation and launched a swift and forceful attack on the front row of snakes, slaying up to ten of them.

They opened an entrance for the Anantha Sena to enter into Cobrython's defensive formation and break it from inside. The soldiers from the mid circle of the Suchakra formation now entered the enemy formation and started attacking from inside. Even though their swords weren't sharp enough to penetrate the snake's skin, they could make huge blows in the enemy's formation as directed by Littpin.

Littpin and her companions showcased their exceptional combat skills by infiltrating deep into the enemy's formation and eliminating multiple Cobras. The decreasing numbers in his army forced King Cobrython to engage in a full-scale battle. He unleashed a barrage of strikes with his tail, resulting in the death of thirty soldiers per strike. In just nine strikes, nine platoons were wiped out.

Additionally, the soldiers inside the Cobra formation suffered heavy losses, with many losing their lives or being paralyzed by the venom. The Chief eventually regained his senses and assessed the situation, prompting him to order the surviving soldiers to retreat back into the Suchakra formation.

All the remaining soldiers fell back, and the size of the Suchakra was considerably reduced. Their number was reduced from twenty-five platoons to fourteen platoons. But Littpin and the five were still inside the enemy formation, deep inside and continuing their kills.

Just as the Chief was considering changing the Suchakra formation, the enemy started launching giant fireballs towards them. In a panic, the Chief ordered a retreat, but many soldiers were killed by the fireballs as they fled. Cobrython's army pursued the retreating soldiers, killing them as they went.

Littpin quickly realized that the fireballs were being launched by the outlaws using catapults from a position behind them. She instructed Dravas to shoot a fire arrow at the outlaw position. The arrow hit its mark, causing a massive explosion that destroyed the catapults and killed many of the outlaws.

Littpin and her team were now the targets of Cobrython's rage. Despite her dodging skills, Cobrython's strikes were relentless. Littpin managed to cut the tip of Cobrython's tail, causing him to scream in agony and prompting the other Cobras to attack.

The battle was intense, and the remaining three soldiers of the Vaani Sena died, leaving only Littpin, Dravas, and the Captain. Surrounded by hundreds of Cobras, they knew a sword fight was not advisable.

Dravas improvised by throwing two pokala on the ground, creating a smoke screen that obscured the snakes' vision. They cautiously tiptoed towards the other side, only to be met by glowing eyes in red and green hues.

"He can see through this smoke." Said Dravas.

Before they can do anything, Cobrython strikes at them, and Littpin, Dravas, and the Captain fall down. In a desperate move, Littpin asks the Captain for the fallen teeth of Cobrython, which he had collected from their first battle. The Captain hands over the teeth to Littpin, and when Cobrython charges at them again, she jumps and pierces the two teeth into his stomach.

Cobrython screams in agony and starts rolling on the ground. Hearing their King's screams, the Cobras rush towards Littpin, but as they get closer, they explode into pieces, shocking Littpin.

Littpin surveyed the battleground and noticed the ground covered in the blood and flesh of the Cobras. Dravas was lying on the ground beside his open small box, and she realized that he used something from the box to kill the Cobras. Littpin had earlier suspected that the box contained something other than tools, as Dravas had claimed.

The Cobras had suffered significant losses, with only about fifty left alive, and the outlaws were also reduced to a similar number. However, Littpin's side had also suffered heavily, with only two platoons of soldiers remaining. She looked at Cobrython and saw that he was motionless.

"The Lord is there with me". She whispered, taking a long breath.

Chapter 56

CHIEF ASHWADARSH

Dravas was injured from the fall, and Littpin rushed to him.

He asked, "It's dead right?"

"Yes, uncle." Said Littpin.

Dravas gazed at the sky, shut his eyes, and let out a sigh of relief,

"My son, we have avenged your death," as tears streamed down his cheeks. He gave Littpin a grateful smile and gently patted her shoulder,

"Thank you, my dear."

With those words, Dravas turned and walked away from her.

The Captain approached Littpin and asked,

"Is that what was written in the scroll?" to which she smiled and nodded.

"Finally, it has ended, King Cobrython and his army," Captain exclaimed.

And then, looking at the remaining outlaws and the Cobras, he shouted,

"What are you waiting for? Come, fight and die."

The outlaws and the Cobras did not launch an attack since they needed their King's command to do so, leaving them stranded.

Littpin and the Captain approached their surviving troops, who appeared frightened and had fear in their eyes. The earlier fireball assault and the Cobras' subsequent strike had left them intimidated, and Littpin realized that the once-mighty Anantha Sena's morale had been shattered by Cobrython and his army.

Littpin understood that delivering another war speech would not uplift their morale. As she searched for Chief Ashwadarsh, she found him absent from the scene. After scanning the surroundings, she realized the reason behind Anantha Sena's crumbling morale.

Littpin hurried to the location and was astounded to witness Chief Ashwadarsh's demise. Dravas and some soldiers were present, standing next to his scorched remains. Littpin was taken aback by the sight - the Chief's legs were entirely burned, and the ash had dispersed with the wind. Half of his face was devoid of flesh, and there were three holes in his upper torso, bearing the bite marks of Cobras. Upon closer inspection, she noticed that the teeth had penetrated much deeper, with remnants of charred Cobra teeth still present in one of the holes.

A soldier who was present at the scene was weeping uncontrollably, he recounted,

"Our Chief engaged in a fierce fight with two Cobras that followed us, and he instructed us to flee while he held off the Cobras, sacrificing his own life to protect us. He was a true leader, and he died to save us." Said the soldier in broken words.

He continued,

"Despite one of the Cobras piercing its teeth deep into his chest, the Chief did not back down. He bravely wielded his sword and managed to sever both of the Cobra's teeth. Though the Cobra writhed in agony, the two teeth remained embedded in the Chief's body, weakening him due to the poison. His legs began to tremble, and he fell to his knees. The other Cobra attempted to attack him, but he countered it by slashing its teeth, causing one tooth to fall off. However, the Cobra managed to pierce the Chief's chest with its remaining teeth, leaving him unable to lift his sword as his strength ebbed away. In a final act of valour, the Chief resorted to his dagger, stabbing the Cobra in its eye, causing it to shriek in pain. Before the scream could subside, a massive fireball descended upon both of them, leading to the Chief's tragic demise...."

The soldier couldn't continue his narration, as his heart weighed heavily with sorrow.

"Long live the chief." Said the Captain after hearing the brave fighting story of Chief Ashwadarsh.

Littpin looked at the Chief's charred body and said,

"Today, he did not pass away, but he engraved his name in history."

Chapter 57
ONE LAST FIGHT

The sound of hissing voices reverberated through Rockhill, causing Littpin to glance in the direction of the Cobras and outlaws. They appeared to be cheering for someone, and upon closer inspection, Littpin realized that they were rallying behind the fallen Cobrython. With a determined expression, Littpin muttered,

"For one last fight."

With a slow, deliberate movement, Cobrython lifted itself up, extending its hood and unleashing a piercing hiss that echoed throughout Rockhill. The mere sight of it caused the remaining soldiers of Anantha Sena to tremble with fear. Fixing its gaze upon Littpin, Cobrython raised its head, baring its sharp fangs in preparation to strike. Sensing the danger, Littpin motioned for Captain and Dravas to lead the soldiers of the remaining two platoons.

The Captain went to the platoon and said,

"I am not going to give you a speech, but one thing, even if we die today, we will die as a hero."

There was a palpable sense of magic in the air that lifted the spirits of the soldiers and rekindled their fighting spirit. Littpin knew that Sajeera, their skilled Captain, was the best at motivating his troops, and she trusted him implicitly. With this in mind, she directed Sajeera and Dravas to take charge of the two remaining platoons of Anantha Sena. They were confident in their ability to lead the sixty soldiers in a successful attack against the Cobras and outlaws. With two seasoned captains at the helm, victory was surely within their grasp.

Littpin was prepared for battle, but to her surprise, Cobrython turned and charged towards the Captain and his platoon. Littpin followed after the serpent. Cobrython knew that destroying the Anantha Sena would not inflict much damage on his army, so he decided to take them out first. Despite the sudden turn of events, the soldiers remained steadfast and were ready to fight to the death.

Cobrython abruptly stopped in front of the defensive formation of the platoon, and began to spin vigorously, then leapt onto the top of the formation, causing nearly fifty soldiers to be thrown to the ground. Without any resistance, Cobrython moved on to attack the remaining soldiers, as well as the Captain.

As Cobrython was about to strike the soldiers and the Captain, he suddenly felt a sharp pain below his neck. He hadn't realized that the eagle pommel sword had made the cut. Littpin had attempted to decapitate Cobrython but couldn't reach the necessary height, so instead, she made a cut just below his neck. Cobrython writhed in agony as blood poured out from the wound. If the eagle pommel sword had been intact during the first fight, Cobrython would not have survived this long.

The Cobrython screamed by opening the mouth of both its head. The sound of Cobrython's dual screams echoed through the battlefield as the Cobras and outlaws cheered and rushed towards Littpin. However, Cobrython gestured them to stop. He was determined to take revenge and kill Littpin personally. In response, Littpin signalled for Captain, Dravas and the soldiers to hold their ground, indicating that she wanted a fair fight.

As Littpin charged forward with her sword raised, Cobrython met her in a head-on collision. The flames from the burning tree illuminated the Rockhill in a fiery red glow, casting an eerie light on their intense battle. Despite Cobrython's best efforts, Littpin successfully blocked all of his attacks, and with each block, she delivered a swift counter-attack that inflicted deep cuts on the King's body. Although Cobrython was bleeding profusely, he refused to give up, and he attempted to wrap Littpin in his powerful tail. However, she managed to dodge the attack and continued to fight.

After Littpin missed her target, Cobrython quickly dodged her attack by curling his tail and bending down. Littpin fell to the ground and dropped her sword. Cobrython then charged at her with full force, but she rolled over and managed to avoid his poisonous fangs. Littpin stood up and tried to retrieve her sword, but

Cobrython struck her with his tail, causing her to fall again. As she lay face down on the ground, she turned her head to see Cobrython up close, sniffing her face. Littpin was filled with anger and vengeance, and Cobrython sensed it.

After raising his head, Cobrython swiftly charged towards Littpin, opened his cobra mouth, and aimed to pierce his fangs into her. However, Littpin kicked Cobrython's stomach and pushed herself away, avoiding the attack. Cobrython's fangs struck the rock, but they remained unharmed due to their strength.

As Littpin charged towards Cobrython with her sword, he awaited her attack and quickly wrapped his tail around her when she jumped towards his head. If she had been on the ground, she could have evaded this move, but she was airborne, making her an easy target. Cobrython had anticipated her move as she always aimed for his head. Littpin raised her sword to shoulder level to prevent it from getting trapped inside the tail, leaving only her torso unwrapped. The rest of her body below her hip was entirely wrapped by the tail, and Cobrython began squeezing her. As her lower body parts were being crushed, she screamed and struggled to strike back with her sword, but she was losing the strength in her hands. The eagle pommel sword fell to the ground, and her vision faded, and she said,

"Father, I am coming."

Chapter 58
THE AIRBORNE

A midst the red atmosphere, she felt a sense of darkness. Memories of her childhood flashed in her mind, and she heard voices in her head as she descended into the darkness. In her mind's eye, she saw a lovely lady in a sky-blue dress, accompanied by Venkad, looking at her with affection and smiling. Suddenly, she found the woman lying on Venkad's lap, covered in blood. Another lady was holding two children, and the woman on Venkad's lap whispered something softly into one of the children's ears. For a moment, it was completely dark and silent.

Suddenly she fell to the ground and regained consciousness. She saw that the Cobrython was airborne.

"He could fly?" Asked Littpin herself.

And with a thud sound, Cobrython fell. Then Littpin realized that Cobrython wasn't flying himself but was lifted by something.

"What could it be?"

"Cobrython itself is huge, and if something could lift him, it might be massive."

"What will it be?"

"Will it be our friend or enemy?"

Her mind was flooded with thoughts, including those about what she had seen in another reality.

"Who was that lady?"

"Who are those two children.?"

"Is she…"

Just as she was about to ask her questions, Cobrython commanded the Cobras to kill Littpin. Up until that moment, Cobrython had intended to kill Littpin himself, but now he had shifted his strategy and ordered his Cobras to do the job. Littpin observed this shift in Cobrython's priorities and understood that she was no longer his primary target

"What could it be?" She asked herself.

Littpin noticed the Cobras aiming at her and attempted to pick up her sword from the ground. However, her body was weak due to Cobrython's squeezing, and she struggled to lift it. Dravas, who was observing Littpin, came to her rescue. He hurled two pokala at the charging Cobras and then took Littpin to the Captain and the remaining ten soldiers.

The heavy smoke from the pokala filled the atmosphere, making it red due to the flames of the tree. The Captain and Littpin were perplexed by the scene before them, but Dravas maintained his composure. Suddenly, they heard Cobrython's loud screams and a thudding sound. Littpin recognized that Cobrython had been lifted again and then dropped by that mysterious force. The smoke, which had been still until then, began to move violently as if a powerful wind was blowing.

The Rockhill fell silent once more, with only the sound of twigs falling from the tree as it burned. As the smoke dissipated, Cobrython's glowing eyes could be seen amidst the haze, searching for something in the sky. Cobrython spun around as well. Suddenly, a piercing screech shattered the silence of Rockhill, and even Littpin and the Captain were frightened by its intensity. It was more terrifying than Cobrython's hissing and screaming.

Littpin was taken aback when she gazed upon Dravas, who appeared tranquil and collected. He met her gaze and grinned, a smile that conveyed multiple meanings, but Littpin couldn't discern any of them. The smoke swirled violently now, as if propelled by an intense gust of wind, while Cobrython gazed up at the sky, and a loud flapping sound reverberated through the air. Littpin was incredulous, and the Captain's mouth hung agape while the soldiers were stupefied.

A huge eagle, nearly ten times the size of Ammu, landed on Rockhill with a rider clad in full body armour and a helmet. Littpin and the Captain were unable to identify the rider, but Dravas smiled at the person, who waved back. Cobrython began hissing at the eagle, which screeched back in response. The rider commanded the eagle to attack Cobrython, and it flew towards the creature, grabbing and constricting its neck with its sharp talons. Cobrython let out a cry of agony, and the Cobras rushed to his defence. The rider then instructed the eagle to take off, still clutching Cobrython's neck with its claws.

Cobrython's demise was seemingly inevitable, yet fate had other plans. An enormous iron net was launched towards the soaring eagle, instantly placing it in peril. The net was equipped with four massive stones, one attached to each corner, and the eagle was unable to sustain the added weight. Consequently, the eagle plummeted downward with Cobrython's neck still clutched between its sharp claws. Littpin searched frantically throughout the Rockhill to determine who had launched the iron net. Her gaze fell upon a modified catapulting machine that had been designed to launch the net and stones. Standing beside the machine were the outlaws, and she was astounded to see that they possessed several more of these nets.

"Did they anticipate this attack from the sky?"

"Who designed these nets?"

"Who modified these catapulting machines?"

She thought.

The impact of the fall was significant, given the weight of the iron net and stones. To mitigate the impact, the eagle had dropped Cobrython before hitting the ground. The rider also fell and suffered damage to their armour. Upon seeing the fall, Dravas hurried to the site to assist. He attempted to remove the iron net, but the stones tied to the four corners made it difficult. He then shifted his focus to pulling the rider out of the net. However, the eagle was still trapped within the net.

As the eagle was trapped in the iron net, Cobrython seized the opportunity to attack Littpin again. She raised her sword but couldn't lift it to her shoulder level, realizing that this was the end. With a quick glance around, she saw the Cobras charging towards Dravas, the rider, and the eagle, while the remaining outlaws were advancing toward the Captain and the ten soldiers.

As Littpin surveyed her surroundings, she noticed that the soldiers had resigned themselves to death; they seemed prepared to die, having already witnessed many terrifying things. They had seen the advanced platoon go up in flames, the Chief's charred remains, and fireballs, among other things. It appeared as if they had made peace with their imminent demise.

Meanwhile, the eagle, whose sudden appearance had given them hope, was now trapped and in danger of being killed by the Cobras. The rider, whose armour had been broken, and Dravas, who seemed to have lost interest in the fight, were both facing the Cobras' charge.

As Littpin faced Cobrython, she saw the determination in his eyes despite his bleeding neck. He knew his revenge was close at hand. Cobrython let out a deafening hiss that echoed throughout Rockhill. Meanwhile, the eagle, struggling to free itself from the iron net, screeched in distress, causing everyone to cover their ears to avoid the piercing sound. Littpin's eyes filled with tears as she watched the eagle fight for its life against Cobrython's attack.

Chapter 59
THE BLUE

With all his strength, Cobrython drove both his fangs deep into Littpin's heart, causing her to fall like a wilting flower from a tree. As she hit the ground, the flames of the tree slowly dwindled, the eagle ceased its screeching, and the battlefield was consumed by an eerie silence upon the hero's defeat.

King Cobrython himself stood motionless upon witnessing her demise. Tears streamed down the faces of Captain and Dravas, both of them mourning over their fallen comrade while the rider struggled to free himself from the iron net. As her vision blurred, Littpin could make out Dravas's tears as he lay on the ground with his arms on his head.

As the eagle struggled, it caused the iron net to loosen at one end, allowing the rider to escape through the gap. She removed her helmet to reveal a lady in a bluish-white dress. Taking off the remnants of her upper armour, a blue pendant on a necklace was revealed around her neck.

As Littpin watched the blue pendant glisten and emit a soft blue light which is coming towards her, she felt drawn to its beauty, and her eyes began to close. Gradually, she slipped into darkness, and once again, she saw the two children and the woman drenched in blood speaking to one of them. The mind voices she had heard before returned, but this time they were crystal clear, and she recognized them as a message from her mother, Bhuvina. She listened intently and slowly started to come back to consciousness.

Littpin opened her eyes and found herself suspended in the air with no apparent means of support. Her companions on the ground, including Dravas, the lady, and the Captain, looked up at her in amazement, their eyes brimming with tears. A blue light enveloped Littpin, giving her bluish eyes and illuminating the entire Rockhill. The soldiers and outlaws present were stunned by this extraordinary sight; they had never seen anything like it before. However, Dravas and Cobrython appeared unfazed, having already witnessed similar phenomena.

Littpin closed her eyes, and a rush of memories flooded her mind - Venkad carrying her to bed, his laughter, his death, the hill climb with Akshuru, Abheera's recruitment test, their conversations, Ammu's reaction upon seeing her, Ammu's lifeless body, Abheera's final cry for help, and Dravas's tears for his lost son.

Her body shook with anger, her hands clenched, and her eyes remained shut. She felt an immense power coursing through her, fueling her thirst for revenge. King Cobrython would soon learn that revenge backed by such strength was a lethal combination.

Dravas, the lady, and the Captain understood that Littpin was angry and her revenge was boiling like a volcano, which would explode anytime.

Littpin opened her eyes; blue wasn't just a colour. It was the flame sourced from her mind; she screamed,

"Cobrython…"

The sound of Littpin's scream reverberated throughout Rockhill, causing everyone to cover their ears and stand still. With her eyes blazing blue flames, Littpin appeared fierce, and even Cobrython was intimidated. However, the snake king remained composed and no longer held any animosity or desire for revenge.

"Cobrython, you killed my father, you killed Abheera, and you killed many innocents. You will not be forgiven. You will reap what you sow." Littpin's voice echoed over the Rockhill.

Littpin's words left the Captain stunned as he realized the immense power she possessed, fueled by the blue light emanating from the pendant. Cobrython stood calmly, observing her, while the rest of the onlookers were in shock.

"But why the blue light passed onto her only? Why not to others?" he thought to himself.

It is well known that Littpin is preparing to face Cobrython in battle. Although her sword is lying on the ground, she shows no intention of picking it up to begin the fight. She looked at Cobrython, and she thundered,

"Sarparna Sthabdh Sthabdh

Chalana Sthabdh Visha Sthabdh

Parvai Sthabdh Chintha Sthabdh

Sarvamaya Sthabdh Sthabdh"

A blue flame entangled Cobrython, and he was lifted from the ground. Everyone was stunned by seeing the power of Littpin.

Cobrython's always moving heads suddenly came to a stop, his sharp fangs dropped, and his eyesight and thinking ability were impaired as he was lifted into the air. Not only Cobrython but all the remaining Cobras were also lifted in the air, unable to move or think.

The Captain now comprehended the reason behind the snakes' reaction to "Sarparna Sthabdh," which was only a fragment of the entire spell Littpin had spoken.

Cobrython and the other snakes revolved in the sky with a blue flame ring around them. Littpin remained up in the sky with her clenched fists. Dravas and the lady in bluish-white dress decided that Littpin had to be stopped; otherwise, she would use any other spell out of her vengeance, which may destroy the whole Bharatha country.

Dravas shouted,

"Littpin, calm yourself. Cobrython has got the punishment. Look at him."

The flame inside her eyes was still burning, and she couldn't reply to anything. She turned towards Cobrython.

The lady alerted Dravas,

"She has to be stopped. She is now possessing enormous powers of the angel clan, and she is not trained to use or control it. She has to be stopped at any cost."

"How will we stop her? She is now blind by her vengeance and will not heed our words." Said Dravas.

Littpin's clenched fists opened, and the eagle pommel sword was lifted by a blue flame, reaching her hands. She raised the sword, and it began to glow in a blue flame as they looked on.

"Stop her, Cobrython has got his punishment, and it is over. We shouldn't kill him." Said the lady.

"But he deserves to be killed." Said Dravas.

"No. You don't know about Cobrython and his past." Said the lady.

"I am not saying that he should be killed. All I said is he deserves to be killed. He has killed Venkad, Abheera and Ammu. What about them.?" Dravas said.

Just as the lady was about to speak, they were shocked to see that Littpin had already begun her next spell. All eyes were fixed on Littpin.

Her eyes were closed, and her blueish-flamed eagle pommel sword was raised to the sky.

"Lokatma mudivu,

Sarvauyiru mudivu...."

Before she could complete the spell, a loud shouting echoed,

"Littpin...no..."

The voice surprised Dravas, the lady, and the Captain. They all turned their attention to the source of the voice. Littpin also directed her gaze towards the origin of the voice as she recognized it.

"Uncle." She said.

Muthu appeared, donning an armour and wielding a sword and daggers, accompanied by another person with bruises on his body and soil-coloured armour, indicating a hard fall.

"Abheera,"

Dravas said, and he burst into tears seeing his son alive. Seeing Abheera alive, the Captain felt like he got his life back. He finally learned what had happened to Abheera on the run - he fell into Ammu's open grave, which had been dug by the outlaws. Abheera was unaware of the open grave.

Littpin's anger subsided after seeing her uncle and Abheera. The flames inside her eyes slowly faded, the blue aura surrounding her was gone, and she slowly landed near Muthu. She dropped her sword and hugged Muthu, and said,

"I missed you, uncle." She burst into tears.

The sudden transformation of Littpin from a powerful being with blue flames in her eyes and sword shouting spells floating in the sky to an ordinary girl weeping under her uncle's shade surprised everyone. Muthu patted her shoulder.

"Uncle, why did you stop me? He killed my father." Said Littpin

"My dear, you have chanted the wrong spell. If you had completed that spell, everyone here, including you, would have died. Your vengeance has blinded you, and also, you are not trained how to and when to use these spells." Said Muthu.

"I don't know, uncle. That blue light from the pendant gave me all this power and my life back." Said Littpin

"The power was always inside you, and this blue light was just a cause that triggered your power." Said Littpin.

She was shocked to hear that,

Littpin asked

"Why do I have this much power, uncle? Who am I? I saw my mother, and It was her voice that was speaking to me all this time. She told me all the spells, uncle. She was bathed in blood; what had happened to her? Who killed her?"

"It's not the time to tell you all those stories. We have to take the Cobrython to the ancient village before it's too late." Said Muthu.

"What about father? He killed father." Said Littpin.

"You already gave him a lifetime punishment, dear. He won't be able to see, move or even think about anything." Said Littpin.

Littpin looked at the revolving Cobrython and his army of snakes. And Muthu continued,

"King Cobrython was a beloved leader of the snakes, and they revered him as their King. One day, two angels were in the forest making love when one of them accidentally stepped on a snake. The snake, in a reflex action, bit the angel in self-defence. Enraged, the bitten angel beheaded the snake. King Cobrython sought justice and went to the angel court, but the angel who killed the snake was arrogant and refused to listen to his plea. They had a heated argument that eventually turned into a fight, and Cobrython killed the angel. The other angel, assuming that Cobrython had killed her lover out of revenge, cursed him and his people, saying that their life would be ruined by Cobrython's revenge."

He continued,

"Cobrython and his snakes went into exile to avoid any further conflicts, and nobody knew where they had gone until General Atheendra's horse was bitten by Cobrython's snakes. However, the curse was triggered when rogue soldiers burned down their settlements, destroying many eggs. Your father sought to sever the connection to the deep forests to prevent any further disruptions to Cobrython's exile."

As Muthu recounted the story of King Cobrython's past, Littpin gazed at him, seeing him spinning in the air with his eyes shut. Tears streamed down her cheeks as she came to the realization that the entire war was not his fault. Cobrython had retreated deep into the forest to avoid any outside contact, and he didn't start the battle that led to his punishment. This realization made Littpin forget about seeking revenge against Cobrython.

Chapter 60
THE VISIONS

Littpin turned to Muthu and asked,

"Mother told me all the spells, but she didn't tell me about any counter spell to revoke a spell. Is it possible that I could save him?"

"No, my dear. The knowledge of a counter spell is exclusive to the leader of the angel clan," stated the lady, to which Muthu nodded in agreement.

"Who is the leader of the Angel clan? We should meet her." Said Littpin.

"You will get to know when it's time; now, we cannot meet her." Said the lady.

"If you can't tell me who the leader is, tell me where the angels live. Where is their place?" Asked Littpin.

"Their leader sealed their location using a spell that can only be undone with a counter spell cast from outside." Said Muthu.

As they were talking, the piercing screech of an eagle trapped in an iron net interrupted their conversation.

Dravas and Abheera hurried to lift the net while Muthu joined in to help. However, they failed to consider the unique abilities possessed by Littpin. Suddenly, before they could reach the net, it was lifted away, and the eagle flew off to freedom. Littpin grinned as the eagle soared into the sky and eventually landed near her. She lovingly stroked the massive bird's belly.

"It likes you." Said Abheera.

Littpin expressed her joy at seeing Abheera alive and tightly embraced him. However, despite his survival, sadness lingered in Abheera's eyes as he grieved for Ammu. It was unfortunate for him to spend an extended period in Ammu's grave pit when her mortal remains were no longer there. Recently, the Captain had informed him of what had happened to Ammu's remains, which had left Abheera feeling distressed.

"Abhi, I missed you a lot. I thought you were gone like my father. But I am fortunate that you are here with me. And hereafter, never leave me." Littpin said.

Because it was after Abheera's missing that Littpin realized how much she liked him.

"I will not." Said Abheera, and he made his way to the corner of Rockhill where the bones of Ammu had been gathered. Despite Littpin's attempt to call him back, the Captain signalled for her to refrain from doing so. The Captain had previously informed Littpin of Ammu's grave and urged her to allow Abheera some space.

As part of the protocol, Muthu and the Captain were surveying the battlefield. While inspecting the area, Muthu noticed a scroll lying on the ground and proceeded to open it, but the Captain interrupted it,

"It was Littpin's, but she was unaware of its presence until it had fallen from her possession."

By that time, Littpin had also reached there; she said,

"It was given to me by a beggar."

"A beggar?" Asked Muthu.

Before Muthu could ask any further, a horn was blown from the valley side, and he said,

"Oh, I forgot it. Our Vaani Sena is stationed below the valley side."

"Yes, I was about to ask you the question, Chief. Why you didn't take the army up here?" Captain asked.

Muthu smiled and said,

"When we reached the bottom of the valley side, I saw the powerful blue aura and realized that the army was not needed here anymore. So, I ordered them to stay put and instructed them to sound the horn. If I did not return after three blasts, they were to march to my location. And now, I must proceed to the valley."

Muthu then departed to the valley side.

Afterwards, Littpin approached the lady dressed in bluish-white attire and focused her gaze on the blue pendant. She tentatively touched the pendant, causing it to emit a radiant glow. The lady smiled and said,

"This blue pendant is from the angel clan, and it was gifted to my ancestors by the angel clan leader. And that is why blue light came to you and triggered your powers."

Littpin was lost in thoughts for a while before she finally posed a question to the lady.,

"I have seen you somewhere, but not sure where."

"Is it so? Can't you recollect?" Asked the lady.

Littpin again thought; she smiled and said

"It was a dream. I was sunken, and you were lifting me from a river."

The lady was stunned by hearing this and said,

"It is not a dream. It's vision."

"Vision? No way. You think it will happen?" Asked Littpin.

"It has already happened." replied the lady.

"Already happened? Without my knowledge?" Littpin was shocked and curious. Because she never met that lady and has never drowned.

"Yes. It happened, but not with you." The lady said.

"Then with whom?" Littpin was confused.

"Kutty", the lady replied.

Littpin was perplexed because if it was truly a vision, it should have happened to her. In the dream, she had drowned in the water, not some unfamiliar girl, and she communicated this to her.

"Kutty is not some random girl. She is your sister, your twin," said the lady.

"I have a sister? That, too, a twin?" Asked Littpin.

Littpin's countenance was filled with joy and curiosity. Though she had longed for a sibling with whom she could share stories and play, luck had not been on her side. However, now, as she mourned the loss of her father, she discovered that she had a twin sister. Overwhelmed with excitement, she yearned to meet her long-lost sibling.

"You cannot leave Cobrython like this, Littpin. You must get him to the Ancient village. He is very vulnerable, and evil forces may kill him to take his powers." Said the lady.

"And what about the safety of Cobrython at the ancient village? There also he is vulnerable right?" Enquired Littpin.

To which the lady replied, "No, my dear. The ancient village has a protector."

"And who is that?" She asked curiously.

"Korangeera." Replied the lady. And she continued,

"A giant ape who was created by the forest clan and the angel clan together."

Littpin was shocked when she heard about the giant ape. The lady realized that Littpin was under stress and that she was trying to recollect something.

Littpin's excitement about her sister came to a stop, and she said,

"Kutty is in danger. We must go there."

"What? What danger?" The lady was tensed.

Littpin stated, "A few days ago, I had a dream where a giant ape kicked me, causing me to crash into a statue, and as a result, a sword fell from it."

"But that is not possible; Korangeera would never do that." Said the lady.

Littpin's voice trembled as she exclaimed, "But that's exactly what I saw!" Only moments ago, she had been thrilled to discover that she had a twin sister, but now her sister was in peril, and Littpin could not go to her aid as she had to accompany Cobrython to the Ancient village. Recognizing the urgency of the situation, the lady summoned the eagle, which swiftly came to her, and she mounted it.

Assuring Littpin, the lady said,

"Don't fret. Your sister is as courageous as you are, and she has reliable allies. Her Appachi and Garuda will always be there for her, just as the Lord watches over you."

With a wink, the lady quickly departed, leaving Littpin with no knowledge of her name.But Littpin was sure about one thing, that the lady loves kutty a lot. Because in the dream, when the lady was afraid for Kutty's safety when she was lifting her up.

"Is this lady, Appachi?" Littpin thought.

Littpin was again perplexed by the lady's departing words, "just as the Lord is there for you." How could the lady have known about the beggar lady and the scroll? This thought troubled Littpin deeply. Later that night, they all decided to stay at Rockhill. Abheera sat next to the bones of Ammu while the Captain lay on the ground, relieved that the war had ended. Dravas and Muthu had already left, leaving Littpin alone to contemplate her thoughts as she sat on a rock.

"Will Kutty be safe?"

"I should have gone with her."

"Does she knows that she has a twin sister?"

"I have to help Cobrython, and I need to find the angel clan leader."

"Why did they lock their place?"

"And it can be opened from outside only, that too with a counter spell."

"Oh no, the counter spells will only be known to the angel clan leader. So, that means she is outside…."

"I have to find her and revoke my spell on Cobrython."

"Why didn't the teeth piercing work on Cobrython? The illustration on the scroll indicated that piercing its teeth would cause Cobrython's demise. Did I misunderstand the interpretation?"

"What about the explosion created by Dravas uncle? What was inside his small box, and why was his blade strong enough to cut the snake's rough skin? What was the material, it looked like an iron sword, but it wasn't iron?"

"I should have consoled Abhi in a better way."

Littpin's mind was filled with a variety of disjointed thoughts.

"Who was the beggar lady?"

"Why did she give me the scroll?"

"And how did she know about Cobrython and its vulnerability?"

Eventually, her thoughts became jumbled and unfocused, and she drifted off to sleep.

By this time, Muthu reached the valley side and instructed the soldiers to set up camp for the night. He then entered the Chief's tent, where a table and chair were waiting. Lighting a lamp, he placed it on the table and requested soup, which an orderly promptly brought. Muthu sat down and began to enjoy the hot, steaming vegetable soup, all the while thinking about Littpin and reflecting on the questions she had asked him at Rockhill.

"Mother told me all the spells, but she didn't tell me about any counter spell to revoke a spell. Is it possible that I could save him?"

"Then who is the leader of Angel clan? We should meet her."

"If you can't tell me who the leader is, at least tell me where the angels live; where is their place?"

Glancing at the cloth bag containing the broken pieces of Littpin's flyer, Muthu took a deep breath. His thoughts then turned to his interrupted conversation with Littpin regarding the scroll.

"A beggar lady gave her a scroll?"

"What will be in it?"

Muthu checked his pockets for the scroll and retrieved it. With the scroll in hand, he approached the table and examined it under the light of the lamp. Upon unrolling the scroll, he realized that it was not a written message but a drawing.

Upon seeing the drawing on the scroll, Muthu was taken aback, as it portrayed Cobrython biting its own body and then lying on the ground. The scroll revealed that if Cobrython were to bite itself, the poison would paralyze its own body, a weakness that only two people in the Bharatha country knew about. Muthu was overwhelmed with emotion; his eyes widened, his hair stood on end, and tears streamed down his face, wetting the scroll. With quivering lips, he whispered:

"Brother…"

LIST OF CHARACTERS

Venkad – Chief of Trade, Tamnat.

Muthu – Warrior, brother of Venkad.

Littpin - Venkad's daughter.

Sugandhi – Venkad's home maid.

Virumen - Venkad's Stable keeper.

Vasaraya – King of Bharatha.

Atheendra – General of Bharatha Army.

Rakarna – Lord of Tamnat.

Ajral – Chief of security, Tamnat.

Marutha – chief of Medicine, Tamnat.

Sajeera – The Captain.

Akshuru – Shepherd Boy.

Dravas – Venkad's friend.

Abheera – Son of Dravas.

Manikta – Lord of Malnat.

Ashwadarsh – Chief of Security of Malnat.

Abhijith Cs

The Rockhill & the Valleyside

KORANGEERA

ABHIJITH CHANDRA

OrangeBooks Publication
www.orangebooks.in

KORANGEERA – PRAISE

"The book "Korangeera" is a thrilling fiction story. I could visualise every scene of the book, and he wonderfully designed the storyline to give the reader a visual treatment. Kutty and her friends were such a beautiful book combo, and I loved their funny and emotional conversations. And also, I am excited to know the mysteries revolving around Appachi, aka Radhamma, waiting eagerly for his next book."

Menaga V. I.F.S.

Madhya Pradesh Cadre

"They say it's his debut fiction novel, but I don't think so. His various innovations, like the stone launcher, Vrithavyuh etc., makes Korangeera a fiction marvel."

Sarath Pattambi

Director, LEAD IAS

"The author's debut novel, korangeera, is an action-packed and an exciting novel to read with, full of suspense and twists. It is in easy-to-read style, and the development of various important characters makes this an interesting read. Fiction genre fans should definitely add this to their reading list."

Dr Krishna Muthu Rajan I.R.P.S.

APO/Madras, Chennai Division

Southern Railway.

"The book "Korangeera" is an interesting and immersive read. The book is so well written that scenes can be visualised very comfortably, and reading the book feels like watching a movie. The book speaks about courage and wisdom shown by various characters at different stages of the book, which inspires the reader to face great challenges in life."

Nikita Agrawal I.R.P.S.

"The author's debut novel was an excellent read. The storytelling was captivating and fascinating, which indulge the readers to intrigue at every moment."

Swetha Chhoriya I.R.P.S.

APO Nagpur.

Featured book @ Orangebooks.

Featured Book

KORANGEERA
By Abhijith Chandra

"Korangeera" is Abhijith Chandra's debut into the world of writing. Every goal achieved has a dream behind it and it is literally true in case of "korangeera". Get ready for an adrenaline surge and let your imagination take you on a rollercoaster with this one. This is just the beginning of a sequel of books to be released by the author. The author visualises his book to be made into a movie one day and is working on it. Also he offers the readers something to look foreword to by releasing the title of his next book "LITTPIN".

Other featured books

Reviews across the world – Amazon.

 Kavya Nair

★★★★★

An amazing adventure
Reviewed in India on 7 April 2022

The book is filled with elements of mystery, myth, thrill, suspense and fantasy. It's narrative tone captures our imagination. This fiction through subtle incidents reflects the social realities of today's world. Impatiently waiting for the next book of the series.

 Krishna

Thrilling story
Reviewed in India on 1 April 2022

Too good plot with lot of twists and turns...never felt like debut fiction and kudos to the author... waiting for the prequel and sequel

 Anantha krishnan

★★★★★ Verified Purchase

Fantasy thriller

Reviewed in India on 12 April 2022

Great fantasy story. Feels like watching a movie. The usage of tamil in between feels like we are watching a tamil movie. After about 15 pages, the story starts unfolding and the ending will really make u wait for next book. Eagerly waiting for the next part.

 YEDHU KRISHNAN R

★★★★★ Verified Purchase

Good read

Reviewed in India on 3 April 2022

A unique approach by the author. It will be suitable for all kinds of readers.

Engaging and worth to read.

 ABHILASH

★★★★★ Verified Purchase

Good read fictional story

Reviewed in Germany on 29 May 2022

The storyline is good and fictional. Waiting for the further editions. Really excited to see what will be the next plot. Little bit disappointed that the book is not having much chapters. Hope further books have more chapters.

Amal Krishna

★★★★★ Verified Purchase

Good read

Reviewed in India on 3 April 2022

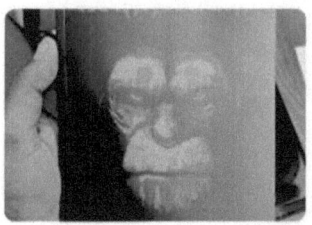

Quick Thoughts and Rating: 5 stars! I would really like to appreciate the young author Abhijith Chnadra for his creativity and imagination. This book, Korangeera gives the chills so many times toward the end. This story can't be categorised as a normal fantasy read as it portrays very relevant subject which deals with current society scenarios. Waiting for the prequel and the sequel.. Kudos Mr. Abhijith.!

 Kiran

★★★★★ Verified Purchase

Engaging

Reviewed in India on 5 April 2022

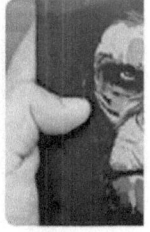

Good read with ample twists and turns. With an apt narration pace, the writter succeeded in maintaining the curiosity and keeps you engaged throughout the book. A well established plot opens the window for couple of installments. Waiting for next one .

www.ingramcontent.com/pod-product-compliance
Lightning Source LLC
LaVergne TN
LVHW091719070526
838199LV00050B/2459